A L

F O

(A Nicky Lyons F… Book
Seven)

BLAKE PIERCE

Blake Pierce

Blake Pierce is the USA Today bestselling author of the RILEY PAGE mystery series, which includes seventeen books. Blake Pierce is also the author of the MACKENZIE WHITE mystery series, comprising fourteen books; of the AVERY BLACK mystery series, comprising six books; of the KERI LOCKE mystery series, comprising five books; of the MAKING OF RILEY PAIGE mystery series, comprising six books; of the KATE WISE mystery series, comprising seven books; of the CHLOE FINE psychological suspense mystery, comprising six books; of the JESSIE HUNT psychological suspense thriller series, comprising twenty-eight books; of the AU PAIR psychological suspense thriller series, comprising three books; of the ZOE PRIME mystery series, comprising six books; of the ADELE SHARP mystery series, comprising sixteen books, of the EUROPEAN VOYAGE cozy mystery series, comprising six books; of the LAURA FROST FBI suspense thriller, comprising eleven books; of the ELLA DARK FBI suspense thriller, comprising fourteen books (and counting); of the A YEAR IN EUROPE cozy mystery series, comprising nine books, of the AVA GOLD mystery series, comprising six books; of the RACHEL GIFT mystery series, comprising ten books (and counting); of the VALERIE LAW mystery series, comprising nine books (and counting); of the PAIGE KING mystery series, comprising eight books (and counting); of the MAY MOORE mystery series, comprising eleven books; of the CORA SHIELDS mystery series, comprising eight books (and counting); of the NICKY LYONS mystery series, comprising eight books (and counting), of the CAMI LARK mystery series, comprising eight books (and counting), of the AMBER YOUNG mystery series, comprising five books (and counting), of the DAISY FORTUNE mystery series, comprising five books (and counting), of the FIONA RED mystery series, comprising five books (and counting), of the FAITH BOLD mystery series, comprising five books (and counting), and of the new JULIETTE HART mystery series, comprising five books (and counting).

An avid reader and lifelong fan of the mystery and thriller genres, Blake loves to hear from you, so please feel free to visit www.blakepierceauthor.com to learn more and stay in touch.

ISBN: 978-1-0943-8161-9

BOOKS BY BLAKE PIERCE

JULIETTE HART MYSTERY SERIES
NOTHING TO FEAR (Book #1)
NOTHING THERE (Book #2)
NOTHING WATCHING (Book #3)
NOTHING HIDING (Book #4)
NOTHING LEFT (Book #5)

FAITH BOLD MYSTERY SERIES
SO LONG (Book #1)
SO COLD (Book #2)
SO SCARED (Book #3)
SO NORMAL (Book #4)
SO FAR GONE (Book #5)

FIONA RED MYSTERY SERIES
LET HER GO (Book #1)
LET HER BE (Book #2)
LET HER HOPE (Book #3)
LET HER WISH (Book #4)
LET HER LIVE (Book #5)

DAISY FORTUNE MYSTERY SERIES
NEED YOU (Book #1)
CLAIM YOU (Book #2)
CRAVE YOU (Book #3)
CHOOSE YOU (Book #4)
CHASE YOU (Book #5)

AMBER YOUNG MYSTERY SERIES
ABSENT PITY (Book #1)
ABSENT REMORSE (Book #2)
ABSENT FEELING (Book #3)
ABSENT MERCY (Book #4)
ABSENT REASON (Book #5)

CAMI LARK MYSTERY SERIES
JUST ME (Book #1)

JUST OUTSIDE (Book #2)
JUST RIGHT (Book #3)
JUST FORGET (Book #4)
JUST ONCE (Book #5)
JUST HIDE (Book #6)
JUST NOW (Book #7)
JUST HOPE (Book #8)

NICKY LYONS MYSTERY SERIES

ALL MINE (Book #1)
ALL HIS (Book #2)
ALL HE SEES (Book #3)
ALL ALONE (Book #4)
ALL FOR ONE (Book #5)
ALL HE TAKES (Book #6)
ALL FOR ME (Book #7)
ALL IN (Book #8)

CORA SHIELDS MYSTERY SERIES

UNDONE (Book #1)
UNWANTED (Book #2)
UNHINGED (Book #3)
UNSAID (Book #4)
UNGLUED (Book #5)
UNSTABLE (Book #6)
UNKNOWN (Book #7)
UNAWARE (Book #8)

MAY MOORE SUSPENSE THRILLER

NEVER RUN (Book #1)
NEVER TELL (Book #2)
NEVER LIVE (Book #3)
NEVER HIDE (Book #4)
NEVER FORGIVE (Book #5)
NEVER AGAIN (Book #6)
NEVER LOOK BACK (Book #7)
NEVER FORGET (Book #8)
NEVER LET GO (Book #9)
NEVER PRETEND (Book #10)
NEVER HESITATE (Book #11)

PAIGE KING MYSTERY SERIES
THE GIRL HE PINED (Book #1)
THE GIRL HE CHOSE (Book #2)
THE GIRL HE TOOK (Book #3)
THE GIRL HE WISHED (Book #4)
THE GIRL HE CROWNED (Book #5)
THE GIRL HE WATCHED (Book #6)
THE GIRL HE WANTED (Book #7)
THE GIRL HE CLAIMED (Book #8)

VALERIE LAW MYSTERY SERIES
NO MERCY (Book #1)
NO PITY (Book #2)
NO FEAR (Book #3)
NO SLEEP (Book #4)
NO QUARTER (Book #5)
NO CHANCE (Book #6)
NO REFUGE (Book #7)
NO GRACE (Book #8)
NO ESCAPE (Book #9)

RACHEL GIFT MYSTERY SERIES
HER LAST WISH (Book #1)
HER LAST CHANCE (Book #2)
HER LAST HOPE (Book #3)
HER LAST FEAR (Book #4)
HER LAST CHOICE (Book #5)
HER LAST BREATH (Book #6)
HER LAST MISTAKE (Book #7)
HER LAST DESIRE (Book #8)
HER LAST REGRET (Book #9)
HER LAST HOUR (Book #10)

AVA GOLD MYSTERY SERIES
CITY OF PREY (Book #1)
CITY OF FEAR (Book #2)
CITY OF BONES (Book #3)
CITY OF GHOSTS (Book #4)
CITY OF DEATH (Book #5)
CITY OF VICE (Book #6)

A YEAR IN EUROPE
A MURDER IN PARIS (Book #1)
DEATH IN FLORENCE (Book #2)
VENGEANCE IN VIENNA (Book #3)
A FATALITY IN SPAIN (Book #4)

ELLA DARK FBI SUSPENSE THRILLER
GIRL, ALONE (Book #1)
GIRL, TAKEN (Book #2)
GIRL, HUNTED (Book #3)
GIRL, SILENCED (Book #4)
GIRL, VANISHED (Book 5)
GIRL ERASED (Book #6)
GIRL, FORSAKEN (Book #7)
GIRL, TRAPPED (Book #8)
GIRL, EXPENDABLE (Book #9)
GIRL, ESCAPED (Book #10)
GIRL, HIS (Book #11)
GIRL, LURED (Book #12)
GIRL, MISSING (Book #13)
GIRL, UNKNOWN (Book #14)

LAURA FROST FBI SUSPENSE THRILLER
ALREADY GONE (Book #1)
ALREADY SEEN (Book #2)
ALREADY TRAPPED (Book #3)
ALREADY MISSING (Book #4)
ALREADY DEAD (Book #5)
ALREADY TAKEN (Book #6)
ALREADY CHOSEN (Book #7)
ALREADY LOST (Book #8)
ALREADY HIS (Book #9)
ALREADY LURED (Book #10)
ALREADY COLD (Book #11)

EUROPEAN VOYAGE COZY MYSTERY SERIES
MURDER (AND BAKLAVA) (Book #1)
DEATH (AND APPLE STRUDEL) (Book #2)
CRIME (AND LAGER) (Book #3)
MISFORTUNE (AND GOUDA) (Book #4)
CALAMITY (AND A DANISH) (Book #5)

MAYHEM (AND HERRING) (Book #6)

ADELE SHARP MYSTERY SERIES

LEFT TO DIE (Book #1)
LEFT TO RUN (Book #2)
LEFT TO HIDE (Book #3)
LEFT TO KILL (Book #4)
LEFT TO MURDER (Book #5)
LEFT TO ENVY (Book #6)
LEFT TO LAPSE (Book #7)
LEFT TO VANISH (Book #8)
LEFT TO HUNT (Book #9)
LEFT TO FEAR (Book #10)
LEFT TO PREY (Book #11)
LEFT TO LURE (Book #12)
LEFT TO CRAVE (Book #13)
LEFT TO LOATHE (Book #14)
LEFT TO HARM (Book #15)
LEFT TO RUIN (Book #16)

THE AU PAIR SERIES

ALMOST GONE (Book#1)
ALMOST LOST (Book #2)
ALMOST DEAD (Book #3)

ZOE PRIME MYSTERY SERIES

FACE OF DEATH (Book#1)
FACE OF MURDER (Book #2)
FACE OF FEAR (Book #3)
FACE OF MADNESS (Book #4)
FACE OF FURY (Book #5)
FACE OF DARKNESS (Book #6)

A JESSIE HUNT PSYCHOLOGICAL SUSPENSE SERIES

THE PERFECT WIFE (Book #1)
THE PERFECT BLOCK (Book #2)
THE PERFECT HOUSE (Book #3)
THE PERFECT SMILE (Book #4)
THE PERFECT LIE (Book #5)
THE PERFECT LOOK (Book #6)
THE PERFECT AFFAIR (Book #7)

THE PERFECT ALIBI (Book #8)
THE PERFECT NEIGHBOR (Book #9)
THE PERFECT DISGUISE (Book #10)
THE PERFECT SECRET (Book #11)
THE PERFECT FAÇADE (Book #12)
THE PERFECT IMPRESSION (Book #13)
THE PERFECT DECEIT (Book #14)
THE PERFECT MISTRESS (Book #15)
THE PERFECT IMAGE (Book #16)
THE PERFECT VEIL (Book #17)
THE PERFECT INDISCRETION (Book #18)
THE PERFECT RUMOR (Book #19)
THE PERFECT COUPLE (Book #20)
THE PERFECT MURDER (Book #21)
THE PERFECT HUSBAND (Book #22)
THE PERFECT SCANDAL (Book #23)
THE PERFECT MASK (Book #24)
THE PERFECT RUSE (Book #25)
THE PERFECT VENEER (Book #26)
THE PERFECT PEOPLE (Book #27)
THE PERFECT WITNESS (Book #28)

CHLOE FINE PSYCHOLOGICAL SUSPENSE SERIES
NEXT DOOR (Book #1)
A NEIGHBOR'S LIE (Book #2)
CUL DE SAC (Book #3)
SILENT NEIGHBOR (Book #4)
HOMECOMING (Book #5)
TINTED WINDOWS (Book #6)

KATE WISE MYSTERY SERIES
IF SHE KNEW (Book #1)
IF SHE SAW (Book #2)
IF SHE RAN (Book #3)
IF SHE HID (Book #4)
IF SHE FLED (Book #5)
IF SHE FEARED (Book #6)
IF SHE HEARD (Book #7)

THE MAKING OF RILEY PAIGE SERIES
WATCHING (Book #1)

WAITING (Book #2)
LURING (Book #3)
TAKING (Book #4)
STALKING (Book #5)
KILLING (Book #6)

RILEY PAIGE MYSTERY SERIES
ONCE GONE (Book #1)
ONCE TAKEN (Book #2)
ONCE CRAVED (Book #3)
ONCE LURED (Book #4)
ONCE HUNTED (Book #5)
ONCE PINED (Book #6)
ONCE FORSAKEN (Book #7)
ONCE COLD (Book #8)
ONCE STALKED (Book #9)
ONCE LOST (Book #10)
ONCE BURIED (Book #11)
ONCE BOUND (Book #12)
ONCE TRAPPED (Book #13)
ONCE DORMANT (Book #14)
ONCE SHUNNED (Book #15)
ONCE MISSED (Book #16)
ONCE CHOSEN (Book #17)

MACKENZIE WHITE MYSTERY SERIES
BEFORE HE KILLS (Book #1)
BEFORE HE SEES (Book #2)
BEFORE HE COVETS (Book #3)
BEFORE HE TAKES (Book #4)
BEFORE HE NEEDS (Book #5)
BEFORE HE FEELS (Book #6)
BEFORE HE SINS (Book #7)
BEFORE HE HUNTS (Book #8)
BEFORE HE PREYS (Book #9)
BEFORE HE LONGS (Book #10)
BEFORE HE LAPSES (Book #11)
BEFORE HE ENVIES (Book #12)
BEFORE HE STALKS (Book #13)
BEFORE HE HARMS (Book #14)

AVERY BLACK MYSTERY SERIES
CAUSE TO KILL (Book #1)
CAUSE TO RUN (Book #2)
CAUSE TO HIDE (Book #3)
CAUSE TO FEAR (Book #4)
CAUSE TO SAVE (Book #5)
CAUSE TO DREAD (Book #6)

KERI LOCKE MYSTERY SERIES
A TRACE OF DEATH (Book #1)
A TRACE OF MURDER (Book #2)
A TRACE OF VICE (Book #3)
A TRACE OF CRIME (Book #4)
A TRACE OF HOPE (Book #5)

PROLOGUE

She had never seen something like this. At least, not in her mailbox.

Agent Nicky Lyons of the FBI peered into the darkness of the long, narrow mailbox at her apartment building, but there were no letters inside. Not even any fliers or spam letters, trying to get her to spend more on things she didn't need. That was what she had expected when she'd decided to quickly check her mail before going up to her apartment.

But no. All she saw was a flat black box... a cassette player.

Something felt off, like she was being watched. Nicky stood up straight, looking over her shoulder and into the lobby of her apartment building. The mail room was just next to the elevators, but it was late now--through the windows, darkness had settled over Jacksonville, and Nicky's neighbors were all in their apartments.

Taking a breath, Nicky knelt down again and looked into the mailbox, half expecting the cassette player to have disappeared. Maybe she had imagined it all; she was tired, and had worked at the office late.

But it was still there, staring at her, waiting for her.

Nicky paused. If there was one thing she knew in life, it was that nothing strange ever happened to her without reason.

She had learned to trust her gut.

And so, she pulled a pair of latex gloves out from her pocket--something she always kept on her as an agent, just in case she ever needed to touch something she couldn't contaminate with her DNA--and reached into the mailbox. Slowly, she removed the cassette player. It was surprisingly heavy; Nicky hadn't seen this old technology in a long time.

She held it firmly in her hands and stared down at the cassette player like it was a bomb. Inside it was a tape. But so many questions flitted through her mind; who put this here? Why?

More importantly: what was on it?

All Nicky had to do was press play, and she'd know the truth.

Nicky's pulse raced, and her palms started to sweat. She knew the contents of this tape could be important, and she had to take it seriously. But at the same time, she was terrified of what she might hear when she pressed play. She was frozen, standing there alone in the mail room of her apartment building, fully aware that she needed to know what was on this. Now.

Nicky took a deep breath and pressed play.

At first, there was nothing but static, but then Nicky heard a faint voice.

"Please..."

A woman's voice.

Nicky's heart sank into the pit of her stomach. The moment felt surreal, but all she could do was listen.

The desperate, whimpering voice continued. "P-please... I don't know where I am... he... he said I have to talk... oh God, I'm so scared. Please, you have to come help me."

Tears instantly burned Nicky's eyes. They dripped down, landing on the cassette player as the reality of what she was hearing set in.

This was no nightmare. And yet the room spun like Nicky was stuck inside of a ride with no way off.

"I'm--I'm scared," the recording continued. "I don't know what to do. I don't know what he'll do to me."

The voice was so desperate, and it was getting harder for Nicky to breathe. She felt dizzy, faint. And yet she couldn't shake the feeling that there was something familiar about this voice, something she'd heard before.

"Please," the voice whispered, barely audible. "If you can hear this... I'm scared. Please, you have to come get me... please, you have to help me!"

A scream erupted from the speaker and made Nicky flinch.

Then, the recording stopped.

CHAPTER ONE

Nicky sat on her couch in her apartment, holding the cassette player and staring at it. She'd listened to the recording a dozen times now, all in an attempt to find something maybe she'd missed--a voice in the background, or any kind of indication as to who had taken this woman, or who she was.

There was nothing. No hint. No clue. Nicky was lost.

Anxiety tore through her as she stood up and paced across her apartment, her hand on her sweaty forehead. Even with the recording off, the woman's voice wouldn't leave her mind.

Get it together, Lyons. The adrenaline was still on high, but Nicky needed to stop thinking and start acting.

She took out her phone and called Chief Franco's personal cell. He would know that if Nicky was calling him on that, it would be important. There was no other reason for him to disturb him so late, but she needed further instruction--clearance to take this thing in and get it examined by techs, forensics, anyone who could possibly identify where it had come from.

The phone rang and rang. Nicky bit her thumb as she paced.

For the past several months, Nicky had been in charge of a task force at the FBI dedicated to finding missing girls--more specifically, there were ten missing girls on the list who the FBI theorized the most likely to still be alive. Nicky and her partner, Ken Walker, had tracked some of them down--they'd managed to get some back alive, but not all could be wins, and this job came with a lot of death too.

To Nicky's great shame, they'd lost more girls on that list than she had ever anticipated. She'd vowed to herself that she'd never let another one die. And although there was a low chance this girl was on the list, Nicky felt that same need to save her.

The kidnapper had chosen Nicky for a reason. He must have known who she was.

I have to find her. It doesn't matter where she is--I have to save her.

Finally, Chief Franco answered the phone. "Lyons, why the hell are you calling me so late? This better be important."

Nicky's jaw tightened. She knew she had to tread lightly with him. "I'm sorry, sir--"

"Don't apologize," Chief Franco said. "Just tell me what you need."

"I... I don't know how to explain this," Nicky whispered, "but I have a recording. I was going through my mailbox and... the tape was in it. I listened to it. It's a girl, Chief, begging for help."

"Jesus," Chief Franco said. "You're not making any sense, Lyons. What girl?"

"I don't know. I have no idea who she is, but someone put this in *my* mailbox."

Just then, Nicky's phone buzzed. She pulled it away momentarily to see a text message--from her contact at the prison, a guard who was overseeing her deal with Fred Garrison--a criminal informant she'd hired on to keep an eye on Felix Anderson, another inmate who Nicky wished wasn't worth the trouble.

Garrison has more info, says it's important. Can you call?

Damn it. This wasn't the time--Nicky had the chief on the line, she couldn't juggle Garrison as well. At the same time, Garrison was a key person to her--she depended on the information he might have to learn more about the identity of the man who had kidnapped Nicky and her sister, Rosie, ten years ago. Nicky had escaped, but Rosie hadn't, and Nicky had been searching for her--and the man who had her--ever since.

Felix knew the identity of the kidnapper. Nicky was sure of it. She'd gotten him to choke up once, confessing that the kidnapper might have been Felix's mentor, teaching him everything he knew about how to kidnap young girls--and get away with it.

Of course, Felix hadn't gotten away with it at all. Nicky and Ken had taken him down.

But Rosie's kidnapper was still at large.

Nicky shook the thoughts away. Why'd this have to come at her now? She couldn't focus on two things at once, so she tuned back into the phone call with the chief.

"Lyons, if what you're saying is true, then this woman's life could be in serious danger," the chief said.

"I know." Nicky swallowed, her throat bone-dry. "I can come right into the office now."

"Do it," Chief Franco said. "We'll get this tape to the lab, and then we'll figure out what to do next. No matter who this girl is, we're not going to stand for this. I'll call the necessary personnel and meet you there."

Nicky's heart raced. Her body felt electrified, like a lightening rod in a storm; she could feel the relentless build of kinetic energy, could sense the impending flash of light and violence about to explode. She hung up the phone and looked out at the windows of her apartment, displaying the skyline of Jacksonville, lit up in the night.

There'd be no resting tonight.

***

Traffic was worse than Nicky expected as she drove through the city under a night sky, only obscured by the slight smog and light pollution. Lights and red brake lights crisscrossed lines of traffic crawling through the city. Nicky felt the rough texture of the steering wheel as she ran her hands along it, her mind swimming.

She hadn't responded to the guard's text about Garrison, and whatever information he had. Nicky had to deal with this first. As important as Rosie was, Nicky's active duty was to the FBI, here in Jacksonville... and someone out there knew who she was, and had kidnapped another woman.

A spine-tingling through occurred to her--the fear that it could somehow be connected. She quickly passed it off. There was no way the kidnapper would send her a tape like that, unprompted, after so many years.

And that was certainly not Rosie's voice on the recording. Although it had felt vaguely familiar, Nicky would know if it had been Rosie's.

Still, Nicky couldn't help but be anxious about what Garrison had to tell her. As she drove, she remembered her phone call with him from the other night, during her date with Ken:

Nicky ran out of the restaurant and landed on the warm street of downtown Jacksonville. The salty ocean air filled her nostrils, mingling with the scents of restaurants, cars, and exhaust fumes. She could hear the sounds of honking horns and voices calling out to one another, but it was better than taking a private call in the middle of a restaurant.

Nicky quickly answered it. "This is Agent Lyons."

"Agent Lyons, this is Brad Barker from the Fillmore Institution," he said. "Do you have a moment?"

"Of course," Nicky said.

"Fred Garrison, one of our inmates, says he has news for you. He wants to talk."

"Right now?" Nicky's pulse had never been louder.

"Yes, ma'am. Is it a bad time?"

Nicky looked back into the restaurant, where she saw Ken sitting there, waiting for her. She bit her lip. She could put this aside for one night, go in there and continue her date...

Or she could seize the chance for answers. If Ken really did care about her and understand her, then she knew he'd understand this, and how important this was to her.

"Now' s perfect. Put him on."

Nicky held her breath as she waited for the voice to come through. Then, she heard it: Fred Garrison. Her criminal informant.

"Agent Lyons?"

"Garrison," Nicky said. "What's going on?"

"I got some information. You said Felix Anderson knows someone you're looking for... a mentor, right?"

Nicky held her breath. This was it. The moment she'd been waiting for. "Y-yes."

"Well, he wouldn't say much on it. I was able to get something, though. It seems the guy still lives in West Virginia."

"Where?" Nicky asked, her heart pounding. "Where in West Virginia?"

"I don't know. There wasn't any natural way for me to ask that."

Nicky's stomach sank. This wasn't enough. She needed an exact location, or a name, or anything that could concretely point to who this guy might be. "I need more than that, Garrison," Nicky told him. "I need a place. A name. Something specific. West Virginia is a big state."

"I know, but that's all I got."

Nicky felt her heart sink. She was close, but not close enough. "Keep trying, Garrison. Get me good information and I promise you'll be out of that prison sooner than you ever imagined."

Nicky snapped from the memory and focused on her driving. She was almost to HQ. Garrison had assured her he'd do his best to get more, and now, late at night, he was randomly trying to reach her.

It had to be important.

The urge to go down to the prison and see him herself made her anxious, but then Nicky thought of the recording. The girl's voice.

Whoever she was, she was depending on Nicky.

The sooner Nicky found that girl and saved her life, the sooner she could deal with Fred Garrison.

CHAPTER TWO

Nicky pulled her car into the parking lot of the FBI headquarters in Quantico, her mind abuzz with anxiety. She was nervous for how the team was going to react to the tape--more than that, she was nervous that it had been found at her apartment. Of course Nicky hadn't asked for this, but it was still an anxiety-inducing process.

The lights in the building were half off, and not many cars were parked in the lot. It was a clear night, and as Nicky parked her car, she took a moment to collect her thoughts.

She breathed in deeply, slowly, and shut her eyes.

The memories of the recording and the voice echoed in her head, but she pushed those away and instead focused on the present. She thought of Ken, his kind eyes, and the way he had looked at her before she left.

For a moment, her heart ached.

She closed her eyes, took a few deep breaths, and asked herself what the best course of action was. She had no idea who was in the recording or why it was in her apartment, but she knew that the only way to find out was to find the girl on the recording and save her.

With a deep breath, Nicky opened the car door and stepped out into the night. The air was cool and still, and the stars twinkled in the sky. A peaceful night to be dealing with something so horrible.

"Nicky?" a voice called out.

Nicky turned to see Ken, walking through the parking lot. Her heart stalled. She knew she was going to see him, but something about the darkness of the sky and the way his dark hair was ruffled, his blue eyes tired and sleepy, made her want to just be with him. But they couldn't; they were at work now, and it wasn't the time for things to be romantic.

"Hey." Nicky hugged herself as Ken approached.

"You okay?" he asked. His voice was gentle, but concerned. "You look like you've seen a ghost."

Nicky nodded, not wanting to say anything for fear of her voice cracking.

"You sure?"

Nicky nodded again, and Ken squeezed her shoulder.

"I'll explain everything inside," Nicky said. "It's... something you have to hear for yourself."

He wrapped his arm around her shoulder, and Nicky allowed herself to relax for just a moment. She didn't have much experience with romance--real romance--but she was getting there with Ken.

The closest thing she'd ever had was probably with Matt, the guy she had been close with in high school, who she'd reconnected with only months ago. But Matt had quickly become overbearing, and Nicky had realized he had no place in her life anymore.

But working with Ken Walker had changed everything. They were more than partners.

Nicky felt safe around him, and she trusted him with her life. She found herself looking forward to the moments when they could just talk and be together--and when he touched her, she felt like she was flying.

Nicky tried to push those thoughts away and focus on the task at hand. She had to be strong and get through the night.

Nicky looked up at him, and smiled. He smiled back, and the two of them walked together into the building.

As they walked, Nicky wondered what the future held for them. Despite the circumstances, Nicky found herself feeling hopeful. She was grateful for Ken's presence, and for his compassion and understanding.

It was moments like these that Nicky knew she wanted to keep in her life.

But as they walked into the building, she couldn't help but look at Ken and feel a warmth inside her heart. He was her rock, her savior, and she knew, no matter what happened, he would be there for her.

They walked towards the entrance, Nicky's mind still abuzz with questions. The building seemed to loom up ahead of them, a fortress of safety and knowledge that could hopefully help them figure out what was going on.

As they walked in through the doors, Nicky felt a wave of nerves wash over her again. She had a feeling they were about to dive head-first into something big, but of course, it wouldn't be the first wild case Nicky and Ken had worked together.

She just hoped this one wouldn't involve losing anyone.

***

The briefing room was completely silent as the recording stopped playing.

Nicky glanced around the table, taking in the reactions of each member of her team. Across from her, Ken sat with a stern look on his face, his dark eyebrows knitted together. He held his interlocked fingers in front of his mouth, making his expression difficult to read, but Nicky knew him well enough to know when he was disturbed by something on a personal level. He'd lost a girl he cared about to violence once, when he was in high school, and he still carried that baggage now that he was in his thirties.

Grace Taylor, the young tech on Nicky's team, had wide eyes and a terrified expression. She covered her mouth with her hands to suppress a gasp.

Meanwhile, Chief Franco--who stood at the head of the table--was merely quiet, taking it in. Listening to something like that had been disturbing for everyone, and even more so for Nicky, even though she'd listened to it so many times already.

"And this was in your mailbox," the chief said.

Nicky nodded, her throat tight. "Yes, Chief. I have no idea how it got there."

"Who is she?" Grace asked, her voice shaky. She had her red hair tied up in a loose bun, like she'd hurried out of bed to get here. Ken looked tired too, with dark circles under his eyes, but he remained quiet, stoic.

"I don't know," Nicky said. "Her voice is familiar to me."

"Me too," Ken said.

Nicky's eyes flashed to his steely blue gaze. Why on earth would this voice be familiar to either of them, let alone both of them?

Nicky racked her brain for the answer. They'd heard it. But where?

Then it hit her. She'd heard this voice before, but not in person. It had been a few weeks ago, while she was reviewing case files with Ken late at night. Case files on the missing girls, the ones they were still looking for. They needed to know who their victims were if they were to save them, and so Nicky and Ken had spent an extensive amount of time merely learning who these women were.

There were four left on the list, four who had not yet been found. Megan Osterlin, Linda Phillips, Delilah Roberts, and Brianna Wilcox.

Four girls with very different lives.

The profession came back to Nicky first: one of them on the list had been a child star, an actor who had once been on television, but after spending her teen years drinking alcohol and absorbing scandals, she'd been reduced to voice work only.

Voice work.

Then, her name:

Delilah Roberts.

Nicky opened her phone, her heart racing. She went to the audio files folder and searched for the recording of Delilah Roberts's voice from a few weeks ago. She tapped the screen and allowed it to play on speakerphone--the same clip she had reviewed with Ken in private late at night.

The recording said: "This is Delilah Roberts, auditioning for the role of Stacey Phelps..."

The voice filled the room, and Nicky saw that Ken was nodding his head in recognition, his expression serious.

The members of Nicky's team looked back and forth between the recording playing on Nicky's phone and the cassette tape they'd just heard playing. The voices were identical; no doubt about it.

Chief Franco's eyes widened as it settled in. "Lyons... this is..."

"Delilah Roberts." Nicky turned off the recording, her mouth bone-dry. She could hardly believe it herself, and yet it was happening. "She's on our list. She's one of our girls."

The room was filled with a stunned silence. The revelation that someone they had been searching for all this time had sent them a message right to their doorstep was almost too much to comprehend. It felt like the walls were closing in, and Nicky could feel her heart pounding in her chest.

Grace shook her head in disbelief, her gaze still wide with shock. "This is insane," she murmured, running a hand through her hair.

Ken, however, kept calm and said, "Okay, so it's Delilah. Maybe this is a good thing. We had no leads to go on, and now we have one."

"It won't be good if she's already dead," the chief said. "And I'm more concerned about how this person found Agent Lyons's personal address."

A chill ran up Nicky's spine as she pictured all the steps the kidnapper would have to have gone through. Finding out her address... sneaking into her building... locating her mailbox...

It should not have been that easy. Nicky had made some enemies in her life. She was only twenty-nine, but she'd been an FBI agent for years now and had arrested a lot of people.

If this kidnapper could hint her down, surely others could too.

I might need to move...

"Well, the details about our task force are somewhat public," Ken pointed out. "Press has covered Nicky and myself before, especially after we saved the vice president's daughter. It's not much, but there are some articles floating around about who we could possibly be."

"If he's a techie," Grace cut in, "he could've cross-referenced Nicky's name, maybe hacked a database to find her address?"

These were plausible explanations, but one thing still didn't add up, and it made Nicky's skin crawl. "But how would he know we were looking into Delilah?"

Silence spread across the room.

"An educated guess?" Grace offered.

Nicky shook her head. "That would be too risky. If he guessed the wrong person, he could have sent this message to the FBI instead. There are hundreds of agents at the FBI, and Delilah is just one woman on a long list of missing girls. There's no way he could have done it with a guess. He had to have known." She glanced at Ken. "You remember viewing the files with me, right?"

He nodded. "All the girls. We've been going through those files for weeks now."

"Then he must have known that we were on to him. And he's been keeping tabs on us somehow. We can't rule out that someone on the inside could have leaked information."

The room fell silent.

Nicky's stomach churned.

I'm being watched...

She looked back at the cassette tape, which was now sitting on the table. Then she looked back at her team--her friends.

"We need to make some moves," she decided, her voice harder than she had intended. "He's made contact. We need to get on top of this."

They all nodded in agreement, but there was an air of unease to the gesture.

Nicky knew what they were thinking.

This was personal now.

Whoever this man was, he'd just crossed a line. He wouldn't get away with this.

"Regardless," the chief said, "we need to focus on Delilah." The chief went into the filing cabinet on the wall and pulled out some files, flipping through them, then came back over, reading it through.

"Delilah Roberts, twenty years old. She's been missing for six months, disappeared without a trace from her home in Miami..."

Nicky, of course, already knew all of this; she had burned all four remaining cases into her mind. With only four girls left to find, she was eager to finish this task force successfully--and see what would happen after.

But she also knew that this was now a personal mission. She had to find Delilah, and she had to find her soon.

"All right, Lyons," the chief said, shutting the file and tossing it on the table, "I'm leaving this in your capable hands. Come up with a game plan. execute it, and find the girl. Ideally alive."

Nicky nodded. "Yes, sir."

Chief Franco clapped his hands together, then headed for the door. "Good luck," he said, and stepped out of the room. The moment the door shut, the pressure hit Nicky; she needed a plan, and all they had to go off was this tape.

"We should take this to forensics," Nicky suggested. "Maybe they can tell us something about the voice, or the content of the message. It's worth a shot."

Ken nodded. "Agreed."

Nicky considered her other options. Someone left this in her mailbox, which meant they would have had to enter her building. This was where Grace came in. Nicky met her eager eyes.

"Grace, I need you to try to pull up surveillance footage from my apartment building and the surrounding area. See if you can figure out who did this."

Grade nodded. "Of course. How good is the security at your building?"

"We have cameras in the lobby and elevator," Nicky said. "But the mailroom... I'm not sure."

"Okay. I'll see what I can do."

Nicky sighed and ran a hand through her hair. She was exhausted, and the thought of this person watching her every move was not comforting. But she had to stay focused. She had a job to do.

Delilah Roberts had a family who was looking for her, a family who cared about her. And Nicky had already lost too many girls on the list. She'd told herself before that even one more would be catastrophic for her--they only had four left. They could save them all.

Including Delilah.

"All right," Nicky said, straightening her shoulders. "Let's get to work."

They all stood up, and Grace zipped out the door. Ken and Nicky lingered behind in the briefing room, and Nicky had tunnel vision--she just wanted to get to forensics now. But Ken's tentative voice stopped her.

"Hey, Nicky." He sounded tender, and she turned to him. The windows of the briefing room showed Jacksonville at night, and the exhausted look on Ken's face reminded her that none of them had gotten any sleep. Nor would they.

Nicky's breath caught as Ken walked closer to her.

"Finding that tape must've been hard on you," he said softly. He reached out and gently brushed a strand of hair from her face. Nicky felt the warmth of his touch, and the kindness in his voice made her heart swell. She imagined the moment she found the tape--her stunned confusion, and how shocked she'd been when she heard the woman's voice. None of it felt real.

"It was," she whispered, barely able to get the words out. Ken cupped her face in his hands and smiled tenderly at her. She could feel the warmth radiating off his body, and before she could stop herself, she was leaning into it--leaning into him--and then he was pulling her close, wrapping his arms around her in a tight hug.

Nicky shut her eyes and melted into Ken's embrace as all the tension drained away from her body; for a few brief moments, they were just two people who had been through so much together, but were still here for each other when it mattered most. She breathed in his scent--a mix of leather and musk--and clung to him tightly, as if it were the only thing keeping them both safe from whatever lied ahead.

She never allowed herself to feel comforted by someone, but with Ken, she'd promised herself she'd try. After their date on the night she spoke to Garrison, they hadn't gone home together--Nicky was too caught up in her mind, and maybe they just weren't there yet. Hell, they hadn't even kissed.

But they were there for each other. And as Nicky pressed her body into his, she was grateful she had him to rely on, not only as her partner--but as something more.

They'd get there in time. They were both broken by their pasts, and Nicky knew Ken didn't want to rush either.

When they finally broke apart, Nicky looked up at Ken and managed to smile. "Thanks, Walker," she said, teasingly nudging him. "You give good hugs."

Ken chuckled and took a step back, looking into her eyes with a reassuring smile. "Anytime, Lyons. Now let's get to work--we'll find this girl."

Nicky nodded. She felt lighter and more prepared for the task ahead. "You're right," she said. "Let's go."

Together, they left the briefing room and headed for forensics.

CHAPTER THREE

Nicky's palms were sweaty as she sat outside of the lab, waiting for the team to come back with news on the cassette. Ken sat across from her, silently waiting, both of them too tired to fill the void of their silence. Nicky was fine with it, anyway. It gave her a moment to catch up with her thoughts.

She wanted to know what Fred Garrison had for her. If he knew the name of the kidnapper who'd taken Rosie all those years ago. This was going to be a continuous distraction, and she wondered if it would be better to get it over with now--but at the same time, if Garrison did have a name, then it would be more painful for Nicky to stay here, instead of flying right down to the kidnapper's house.

Both outcomes were not ideal, but maybe if she had an idea of what to expect, it would ease her mind. She took out her phone and texted the prison guard, Brad, who was her line of communication with Fred until she could speak to him on the phone or in person. She texted back:

Busy, on a case. What does he have?

Swallowing, she tucked her phone away. She could check it later.

Nicky felt Ken's eyes on her, and she looked up to meet them. "Everything okay?" he asked.

Ken had a general idea about Nicky's criminal informant in the prison, and he knew about Rosie and everything that had happened. In truth, he was one of the only people Nicky could trust.

"Garrison might have something more for me," Nicky explained. "About the guy who took Rosie and I. But I don't know what it could be, and I don't want it to distract from the case."

Ken nodded in understanding. "That's a lot to carry around with you, but I'm here if you need me. Just... let me know where you're at, mentally, if things get hard."

Nicky smiled, grateful for Ken's support, even if it did make her feel vulnerable. She didn't like feeling exposed, but she was trying to open up to Ken and accept him as more than her partner.

Before either of them could say any more, the door opened and the forensics team came out. Nicky and Ken rose from their seats in anticipation.

The lead forensics technician, a woman named Sarah, took off her glasses and looked at them both. "There's no DNA on the box."

Nicky's chest dropped. Damn it. She had been hoping for something, and they still hadn't heard from Grace. Her mind raced as she considered her options.

Earlier, Nicky had listened to the recording over and over, trying to see if there was anything she could extract from it using only her ears. But that wasn't enough. They had the right technology here to isolate sounds, and that sounded like the best course of action.

"Can we take this for audio analyzing?" Nicky asked.

Sarah nodded. "I was thinking the same thing. Follow me."

As Nicky and Ken followed Sarah into the forensics lab, her eyes widened as she took in the sparkling array of equipment - including complex microscopes, advanced machines for DNA sequencing and analysis, and monitors with intricate programming for audio analysis. She was amazed by the sophistication of the technology that surrounded her, and by the depth and breadth of what could be achieved here. The air carried a faint hum as electricity flowed throughout the lab, powering all the technology.

"This way," Sarah said, ushering them into a room at the back of the lab. Inside it were several computer screens. Sarah sat down in front of one while Nicky and Ken stood back. She began typing away as she said, "We already loaded the audio into a digital file so we can isolate the sounds on the computer."

Nicky nodded. "Can we tune out the woman's voice and see what's in the background? I thought I could hear static, but it wasn't clear."

Sarah smiled. "That's what we're going to do. We can use a program to reduce the volume of the woman's voice, and then amplify any other sounds that are in the background."

She began typing quickly, and soon Nicky heard a low hum coming from the speakers. Sarah adjusted a few more settings and suddenly, static filled the room.

"Hold on," Sarah said. "Now we just need to adjust the sound..."

As Sarah adjusted the settings, the static began to fade away until all that was left was a low rumble of background noise. But then something else emerged--faint music playing in the background of the recording. It sounded light, like a ukulele, with light vocals--a man singing.

Nicky's spine crawled as the eerie tune played. All three of them remained quiet, listening. Nicky didn't recognize the song. When she'd first heard the recording, it had sounded more like white noise in the background, but now she could hear it loud and clear.

The recording ended, and they all took a collective breath. Nicky shared a disturbed look with Ken. While Delilah had been begging to be spared, the kidnapper had this calm music playing. It would sound nice, if not for the context of the situation, which gave the tune a whole new meaning.

"Very creepy," Sarah muttered.

"I've never heard it before," Nicky said. "Can we run the song through the system and see if we get any matches?"

Sarah nodded. "Sure, I can do that." She began typing away, and soon the song was running through the database. After a few moments, Sarah's eyes widened as she read the screen. "It looks like we have a match," she said. "It's 'Island Nights' by Joe Rockwater."

"Who the hell is that?" Ken asked.

Nicky shrugged. She had never heard of it. She took out her phone and typed him into her search engine, quickly yielding a result. A photo showed a man with sunglasses, tanned skin, and dark hair, smiling at the camera and wearing a Hawaiian shirt. According to his bio, he was forty-six years old and was a local artist from the Bahamas.

That was oddly specific. Nicky checked Joe Rockwater's online presence only to see he had barely any social media followers at all--only a few hundred.

This was not a big name artist. Another scroll through found he exclusively played at live venues and at resorts in the Bahamas, on an island called Wahoe Bay.

"So he's a local musician on an island called Wahoe Bay," Nicky relayed. "A small place, not nationally known, but still with a tourism industry."

"A niche artist, then," Ken clarified.

Nicky nodded, her throat tight. "It doesn't look like Joe's reach has gone beyond this Wahoe Bay place. Is it possible this is where the recording was taken?"

"The Bahamas?" Ken asked. "Delilah was kidnapped in Miami."

"You can get to the Bahamas from Miami by boat in about two hours," Nicky pointed out. "It's not totally impossible."

Ken frowned, his skepticism clear. "It's a stretch to think a local musician from an island would be involved in a ransom situation in Miami. This could be a coincidence."

Nicky's heart sank. She had been so sure that this was a lead. Now, she wasn't so certain. She tried to think of another way to prove that Joe Rockwater was linked to the kidnapping, but came up empty.

Still, something about this whole thing felt off. She was sure that the music had been connected to the kidnapping in some way, but the evidence seemed too circumstantial. It was hard to believe that this obscure musician from a remote island could be linked to a crime in Miami.

And yet this was the only inkling of a lead they had.

"Do you have any better ideas?" Nicky asked Ken. "We can get a flight to the Bahamas within a few hours, just to talk to this guy and see what his deal is."

Ken sighed, rubbing his chin. He didn't seem convinced, but he didn't have a better plan either. After a moment, he nodded. "I guess it's worth a shot," he said.

Nicky nodded. It was worth a shot, at the very least. If she was wrong, then they could handle it, but Nicky had learned to trust her gut in this business.

She understood Ken's skepticism, though. As her partner, he'd always been a good voice of reason--someone to offer up an alternate perspective. As much as Nicky had learned to trust her gut, she'd been wrong before too. To be a good agent, she needed that balance, and she needed Ken.

Nicky had never had this kind of trust and chemistry with any partner.

She had learned to rely on Ken, and appreciate him. After all, without him, she wouldn't have been able to get this far in her investigation. She was grateful for his presence and his willingness to take a chance on her hunch.

Nicky smiled to herself, feeling a wave of appreciation for her partner. She knew he was the perfect person to have by her side. He was smart, brave and eager to take risks. He had her back, no matter what.

"Thanks, Walker," she said with a smirk. "Looks like we're taking a trip to the Bahamas."

Ken sighed, exhaustion written all over his face. It was still the middle of the night, but this was the path they'd both chosen in life. Being an agent meant making sacrifices, and often, those sacrifices were one's sleep.

"I'll book us a flight and meet you at the airport," Nicky said. "Pack light."

Ken nodded.

To the Bahamas, it was.

CHAPTER FOUR

Nicky watched as the plane flew through the sky through the window seat, the bright light of the early morning sun illuminating everything in its path. The sky was a deep navy blue, stretching out for miles, dotted with clouds that twinkled like silver stars. She could see her reflection in the window, the determination on her exhausted face a reminder of why she was here.

The Bahamas was close. And with any luck, Nicky could find Delilah Roberts there. Alive.

Inside the plane, Nicky could hear the faint hum of engines, and the occasional chatter of other passengers as they flew toward their destination. The air outside was silent, punctuated only by the gentle roar of the plane passing through it.

Beside her, Ken quietly flipped through the case files, and Nicky pulled her gaze from the view outside and back to her lap, where she had Delilah's case files open as well.

It was a sad story. As a young girl, Delilah had dreamed of being an actor, as was shown in her many appearances on TV as a child. But the file also stated that her mother was an alcoholic and her father had left when she was young, so Delilah's home life was unstable, and her mother seemed to push her to do a lot more work that wasn't in her range of interest.

By the time Delilah was a pre-teen, she had appeared in more commercials than TV shows, and not many people wanted to hire her. Delilah developed a drinking habit when she was in her teens and apparently didn't have the "look" to be on film anymore, not even commercials, and so she started doing voice work, which was her career up until she was presumably kidnapped six months ago. The circumstances of her disappearance were unclear, but Delilah's friends and family insisted she hadn't run away. Two months after her disappearance, a strange post was made to her social media. Nicky had reviewed this file many times, but she stopped on the printed off screenshot of the post, and with this new information, it sent a chill up her spine.

The post was a black square with the caption "soon, you'll hear me."

This had alerted her friends and family, and the police had sent the case to the FBI--earning Delilah a spot on Nicky's list.

They'd believed she could be alive, but had no idea where, or who'd taken her, or if she had been taken at all.

But now, they had the proof in the recording. Delilah was alive--or at least, she was when that was filmed. And Nicky was going to find her.

Nicky sighed, feeling the weight of the case pressing down on her. She wished she could have done more to find Delilah sooner--the stakes felt higher, and more personal, than ever. After all, this recording had been delivered right to Nicky; she'd been chosen to do this, and if she couldn't save the girl, she wasn't sure if she'd be able to live with it. She wasn't sure if she'd deserve a spot as the head of this task force that was meant to save lives, not lose them.

It seemed that this musician in Wahoe Bay might be their best lead yet. They had another thirty minutes at least before they'd land in the Bahamas, and so Nicky had too much time to build anxiety about it all.

She felt the plane jostle as they flew over a patch of turbulence, and she closed her eyes, feeling the fear take over. Would this be the case that would break her?

What if she couldn't find Delilah? What if the evidence wasn't enough? What if the musician wasn't involved in the kidnapping at all? With each passing second, Nicky's doubts grew and she felt her stomach twist with nerves. She had no idea what was waiting for them in the Bahamas, but she knew that the future of Delilah's case rested in her hands.

Nicky glanced at Ken beside her, hoping to distract her mind. "What do you make of all this?"

He flipped another page, not looking up. "I think this Joe Rockwater guy might have some explaining to do. He's got a record."

Nicky's heart pulsed with hope. If Joe had a record, then it was more likely he could be a viable suspect. Maybe this wouldn't be such a waste of time.

"Shit," Nicky said. "What'd he do?"

Ken sighed. "Theft. He stole money from some tourists. He was arrested a few months before Delilah went missing, and he's been living in Wahoe Bay ever since. Only had to do community service."

Nicky frowned, her heart racing as she processed this new information. Joe Rockwater had a record for theft--did that mean he'd taken Delilah? He had a criminal record, but that didn't necessarily mean he was guilty of kidnapping Delilah or anything else related to her disappearance. But it did make him a suspect, and Nicky knew that if she wanted to find Delilah quickly, she'd have to start by looking into Joe Rockwater more closely.

She couldn't shake the eerie sound of his music playing in the background of the recording. It was so mellow, so lighthearted, for such an awful situation. How could someone play that music, while also holding a woman hostage who was begging for her life?

"What else do we have on Joe?" Nicky asked, rubbing her forehead from the stress.

"Lead singer of a band, mostly play at the resort bar in Wahoe Bay... lives alone. No wife, no kids."

Nicky nodded. On a hunch, she took out her phone and searched up the resort bar, which was called The Sea Farer. It had positive reviews, and Nicky clicked on them. Mostly five stars and four stars... until she started seeing some lower ratings.

Nicky frowned. Someone named Amber left a one-star rating on the bar with the review: *"Hire less creepy musicians! The lead singer of their local band is a total freak! He tried to grope me as I walked past him... horrible experience!"*

Nicky's stomach knotted. It seemed Joe Rockwater had a habit of taking things that didn't belong to him.

"I just don't get it," Ken said, and Nicky looked at him. His brows pinched as he said, "Why send the tape now? Delilah went missing six months ago. And why send the tape at all?"

Nicky thought back to the post on Delilah's social media. They could easily assume it wasn't posted by her, but by the kidnapper. The caption "soon, you'll hear me"... was it really about Delilah?

"Maybe he wants to be heard," Nicky suggested.

Ken nodded slowly. "Yeah, sure, but what's his motive? I mean, he kept Delilah alive for six months... why not just keep her and never contact anyone? Why send the tape?"

Nicky thought about it. Maybe the kidnapper wanted attention--not just from the people who knew Delilah, but to be heard and recognized by a larger audience. He could have been looking for fame or notoriety in some way.

Or maybe he was trying to make a statement of some kind -- he had taken something precious away from someone, and now he was sending proof that she was still alive as a demonstration of his power over her life. He wanted to show that even with all the resources available to her family and friends that they still couldn't save her without him giving them permission.

Then again, if it were all for attention, then why would he send it to Nicky, and not the press?

And how did he even know who Nicky was?

Her spine crawled again. "I don't know what he wants. But I want to know how he knew about me."

"So do I," Ken said. "Grace's theory that he could be a hacker of some kind might be sound. He wouldn't be able to breach the FBI's database, but if he saw your name in the press and knows you're looking for missing girls, he could have breached the post office or something to find out, at the very least, where your mailbox is."

Nicky shivered and sank in the seat. No matter what the answer was, they needed to find this guy.

She checked her phone again. There was still no message from the prison guard about Garrison, and no news from Grace about the security cameras, either. Nicky felt like this plane was purgatory; she could do nothing other than wait for the next move.

She rested her head back on the seat and closed her eyes. For just a moment, she allowed herself to imagine a world where maybe, Fred Garrison could actually give her information on Rosie's kidnapper.

If that were the case, then Nicky would be closer than ever to answers.

It had been ten years since the incident, since Nicky and Rosie had both been taken... but Nicky got away. Nicky wondered if this guilt would ever pass. Even if she did find Rosie--if she found her dead or alive--would it be better?

If Rosie was dead, then Nicky would be left with the guilt of knowing, without a doubt, she had left her sister to die.

If Rosie was alive, then Nicky would know that she left Rosie with a madman for a significant chunk of her life. Would Rosie forgive her? Would she even be able to recognize her? What kind of person might she be?

Would she resent Nicky for not finding her sooner?

No, Nicky was getting ahead of herself now. Hoping too much.

There was no guarantee Rosie would be alive. In fact, it was highly unlikely she was.

Still, Nicky had to hope, even though in the end, it could make everything worse. She made a note to call Dr. Graham, her psychiatrist, soon, to help sort this all out. She needed to be prepared for the worst.

The plane began to descend, the bright blue waters of the ocean sparkling beneath them. Nicky glanced out the window, her heart racing. This was it. This was their chance to find Delilah and put an end to her terrifying ordeal.

"We're almost there," Ken said, his voice low. He put his hand on Nicky's arm, squeezing it gently.

"We'll find her," he said. "We won't stop until we do."

Nicky nodded, her throat tight. She hoped Ken was right. If not, there might be a monster living in Wahoe Bay--and for all they knew, Delilah might not be the only victim.

CHAPTER FIVE

He had never been heard by anyone before.

A man who no one saw, who no one listened to.

But now, he would force them to hear him. They would listen--and they would listen good.

He smiled down at the woman, tied to a chair, her head hanging low. Delilah. What a lovely name, and what a lovely voice.

He towered over her, but she refused to look at him. To get her attention, he tapped on her chin, causing her to look up at him with desperate, pleading eyes. He smiled down at her and took something out of his pocket--a phone.

Her phone.

She gasped, tears brimming from her eyes. "P-please... you can let me go now. I won't tell anyone what happened, I--"

He held up a finger, shutting her up. She'd been with him for long enough now to know when to talk, and when to be silent.

With a grin, he dangled the phone above her head. She merely looked up at it, biting her lip. She couldn't stand, not with the way he'd restrained her. She'd never be able to reach the phone.

He silently taunted her, his eyes sparkling with delight. He knew what she wanted--he could see it in her eyes.

But he wasn't going to give it to her. Not yet. Instead, he began to walk around the room, his feet making a soft thud on the floor and his hands tracing along the walls as if they were made of silk. Delilah stayed quiet as he made his way to the back of the room, where his latest addition was also tied to a chair--but she hadn't woken up yet.

He stopped in front of the new woman, whose name he hadn't learned yet. She was dirty and grubby, a homeless woman he'd snatched up off the street. Her body was slumped in the chair, her head bowed forward and her clothes torn and frayed. She was dirty and disheveled, her skin a pale yellow from the lack of sun. Her thin frame was engulfed by a ratty hoodie, her long hair matted to her back.

No one would even notice this one missing. That was good.

He kicked at the woman's shin, and she startled awake. Her eyes bulged from her skull as she took in the room, then landed right on him.

"What the hell is going on?" she demanded.

He shrugged at her, no words to say.

The homeless woman scowled at him, her eyes blazing with anger. "Let me go!" she shouted. "Let me go right now or I'll call the police!"

He stared at her for a moment, then slowly shook his head. He would not be swayed by her words. She was here now, and he wouldn't give up the pleasure of having her--not yet.

"Say something, you freaky bastard!" the woman screamed at him. "Where am I? Who the hell are you?"

The man just stood there, silent. He wouldn't answer her questions, only taunt her with his presence. He wanted to see how far she'd go--how long she could keep up the fight before giving in and accepting that he was in control of this situation.

He remained still, a smirk playing on his lips as he watched the woman struggle against the restraints. She had no chance at escape; she was completely helpless against him and his power.

"Just give up," Delilah whimpered from across the room, and the homeless woman's head snapped to her.

"What the hell is this?" the woman said.

"You have to accept it," Delilah said. "You have to."

The man smiled. He'd taught Delilah well. She was using her voice for good, on behalf of him. He would reward her for that later.

The homeless woman would learn soon enough.

But now that he'd taken a second voice, he had to ask himself... was it truly enough?

He wasn't satiated yet.

He thought of the possibilities--the thrill of taking a third victim, the joy of having more power and control. He could feel it in his bones, that rush of adrenaline coursing through him as he thought about it.

He looked around the room, his eyes lingering on each woman before finally settling on the homeless one. She was still struggling against her restraints, fighting against her fate with all she had left.

But it was useless.

The man smirked as he stepped closer to her, watching her closely as he contemplated taking a third victim. He knew that if he did, this would be something he'd never forget--something that would stay with him for the rest of his days.

He felt a strange sense of pride swell within him at the thought; a feeling of accomplishment and strength that only came from dominating another human being.

His eyes lit up with evil glee as he made his decision. Yes, it was time for another one.

CHAPTER SIX

The sun had risen by the time Nicky and Ken landed in the Bahamas, and now they were driving along the road to Wahoe Bay in the rental car that had been waiting for them. The sun shone brightly off the crisp blue ocean, illuminating the vibrant green foliage and white sand beaches as Nicky zipped the car up the road.

She had only been to the Bahamas once, years ago, but she had never been on this island. It was small compared to some of the other islands, but big enough to warrant a long, winding road that would lead from the airport, through the town, and toward the resort. Nicky squinted into the sun as she drove, trying to stave off her nerves.

Somewhere on this island was Joe Rockwater, maybe holding Delilah hostage.

They passed through a small suburb with colorful houses. The salty tang of sea air permeated everything, combined with a sweet scent of blooming flowers and freshly cut grass. A hint of coconut wafted in from somewhere nearby, along with a hint of food cooking in nearby restaurants as they passed. Locals wandered the streets of this area, but Nicky knew that as soon as they got to the resort, it would be nearly all tourists.

They drove on in silence, the only sound the wind rustling through the trees and the occasional car passing by in the opposite direction. Nicky's grip on the wheel tightened, her knuckles turning white.

She had to save Delilah. She had to make sure that the kidnapper never hurt anyone again.

Nicky knew it was impossible to save every person on the planet, or even every person on her list. Hell, she'd already lost too many, but she was determined to never lose any more. She might not be able to save every girl in the world--but she could try her hardest to save every girl who this son of a bitch tried to hurt. That was all she could do. One case at a time.

She glanced at Ken in the passenger seat and knew he felt the same way. Since he'd lost his high school girlfriend to a murderer, Ken knew more than anyone how much it hurt to lose someone and not be able to save them. Like Nicky with her missing sister.

"Hey," Nicky said, but kept her eyes on the road, and Ken looked at her. "How do you cope with knowing you can't save everyone?"

He shrugged and ran a hand through his hair. "It's not easy. But I try to focus on the people I can save. The people I can help. I try to make a difference, even if it's just in a small way."

He paused and looked out the window, watching the scenery go by. "I guess I just try to keep going and do the best I can. That's all you can do, really."

Nicky nodded, feeling a little bit better. He was right. There was no point in worrying about the people they couldn't save--they had to focus on the ones that they could. She had to stay focused and do whatever it took to save Delilah.

"You're too hard on yourself sometimes, Lyons," Ken said, and Nicky glanced at him. She knew he was right, so she laughed a little.

"Yeah, I know," she mused. "I can't help it. It's just the way I am."

"Because of your sister," Ken said, and Nicky stiffened. "You blame yourself for what happened to her."

He wasn't wrong. Mostly because it was Nicky's fault, in some ways. She had left Rosie with the kidnapper and fled. She'd dedicated her life to trying to make up for that moment, but nothing ever would.

"You're not wrong," Nicky said. "I do blame myself for what happened to my sister. But I'm trying to make it right. I'm trying to save Delilah, and all the other girls who are in danger. I'm going to do whatever I can to make sure this never happens again."

Ken reached over and squeezed her shoulder. Nicky felt the warmth of his touch and smiled. She was glad he was here with her.

"I know you will," he said. "You're brave as hell, Nicky. Bravest woman I've ever known."

Nicky felt her cheeks heat up at the compliment, and she smiled.

"Thanks," she said. "But I'm not brave. I'm just trying to do the right thing."

Ken shook his head. "You can call it whatever you want, but I know that you're brave. You always have been."

Nicky couldn't help the smile that spread across her face. She was still scared, but she felt a little bit better knowing that Ken was here with her.

After a few more turns, they arrived at the resort, and Nicky pulled the car into the parking lot. She and Ken stepped out and surveyed the grounds. The resort was sprawling, with lush gardens and a large pool in the center. The buildings were a mix of old and new, with a few restaurants, a bar, and a gift shop.

The resort was sprawling, with trees laden with flowers and rose bushes, an Olympic-sized pool in the center surrounded by tall palm trees, restaurant buildings in a mishmash of modern designs and ancient architecture. The air smelled of chlorine from the pool and wafted through the trees from the nearby ocean. The buildings were a mix of old and new, with a few restaurants, and then, of course, the bar.

A large sign that said SEA FARER BAR and an arrow pointed along the side of the resort. The bar was open to the public as well, and it looked like the path would take them right there.

Nicky looked at Ken, who nodded back at her.

"Let's go," she said, and they began walking towards the bar.

The path through the resort was winding and lined with tall palm trees that cast long shadows on the ground as Nicky and Ken walked. They passed a few other people along the way, but no one seemed to pay them any attention. When they arrived at the bar, they saw it was bustling with activity.

The bar was an open-air affair, with tables scattered around a large central area where people could sit and drink or talk in groups. There were several clusters of people around the area, some playing pool or darts while others just talked amongst themselves and drank early morning drinks. A live band played reggae tunes from a stage near the back wall of the building--the same stage Joe would play on. But there was no sign of Joe anywhere. They must have hired many different acts, and it seemed like Joe mostly played gigs for the evening crowd. Nicky wasn't all that surprised to see the bar busy this early, considering everyone here was on vacation.

Nicky and Ken exchanged glances before heading inside, pushing their way through throngs of patrons to the bar, where the bartender--a young man with tanned skin and dark hair, wringing out a glass--was standing.

His eyes locked on Nicky when she walked up. Both Nicky and Ken were dressed lighter than usual for the weather, but Nicky still wore slacks and a button-down white shirt that was more formal than the bikinis and sundresses most women in the bar were wearing. Neither she nor Ken looked like usual customers, and the bartender seemed to pick up on it immediately, because a look of shock took over his expression.

"Can I help you?" he asked.

Nicky subtly flashed her FBI badge, along with Ken. The bartender's eyes widened.

"I'm Agent Nicky Lyons with the FBI," she told him, keeping her voice low. "We're looking for Joe Rockwater."

"Joe Rockwater?" The bartender frowned. "You mean that musician? He's not here... is he in trouble?"

"No," Nicky said, "we just need to talk to him. We've heard some rumors that Mr. Rockwater has been making tourists uncomfortable, and we wanted to verify these claims."

For now, this was a better cover--she didn't want to outright say Joe was a suspect in a serious kidnapping investigation.

The bartender shook his head. "Yeah, Joe's been known to make the ladies uncomfortable," he said. "He has a bit of a reputation for being overly flirty and aggressive with the women here--a lot of them don't like it. But I've never seen it myself. I'm usually on the day shift."

"So why keep hiring him?" Ken asked.

The bartender glanced around, looking uncomfortable. "Well... look, it's not my call, but Joe brings in a good crowd too. There have just been a few incidents with the girls, but ultimately, we only have so many good local musicians on Wahoe Bay, and Joe's one of them."

"So he's popular around here," Nicky clarified.

"Oh, yeah, people love him," the bartender said. "I don't know if we'd get as much nighttime traffic as we do without him. There are other bars around here that are way fancier."

Nicky nodded, and then gestured to the security camera in the corner. "Do you have footage of Joe's last gig here?" she asked. "It might help us understand what happened."

The bartender seemed hesitant at first, but then he sighed and nodded. "Yeah, sure," he said. He motioned for them to follow him around the bar, where he pulled out a laptop from beneath the counter and connected it to a USB drive. After a few clicks of his mouse, a video began playing on the screen--it showed Joe performing on stage with his guitar for an enthusiastic crowd of tourists. Nicky watched intently as Joe interacted with the audience, taking requests and even shaking hands with some of them before continuing his set.

After a few minutes, Nicky noticed the camera angle changed, and her heart skipped a beat when she saw what was happening. Joe had moved off the stage and was now sitting with a woman at one of the tables near the bar. He was leaning in close to her, whispering something in her ear as he put his hand on her shoulder. The woman looked uncomfortable, and she quickly stood up and backed away from him before turning to walk out of the bar.

Nicky felt anger boiling inside of her--this was exactly why they were here. Did Joe do this to Delilah in Miami when he kidnapped her? Did he try to charm her at some bar, then strike when she least expected it?

"This does look bad," the bartender admitted. "We've had some complaints, but I swear I've never seen him hurt anyone."

Nicky nodded, then looked back at the video. "How long has Joe been playing here?" she asked.

"Oh, it's been a few years now," the bartender said. "He's got quite a following here in Wahoe Bay."

Nicky nodded. That seemed to be a given. But there was something else she wanted to know. On a hunch, she took out her phone and brought up a photo of Delilah. She showed it to the bartender. "Have you seen this woman?"

The bartender shook his head. "I don't know... we see a lot of people here."

Nicky nodded, disappointed. She was hoping the bartender might recognize Delilah, but it seemed like a long shot. If Joe did have her here, he probably kept her locked in a room or basement somewhere.

"Do you know where Joe lives?" Ken asked the bartender.

The bartender hesitated for a moment, before finally nodding. "Yeah," he said, quietly. "I know where he lives." He wrote an address on a piece of paper and handed it to Nicky. "But you didn't get this from me, okay? I don't want any trouble with Joe."

Nicky nodded, taking the address and tucking it away in her pocket. "Don't worry," she said. "We'll take care of this."

With that, she and Ken left the bar and headed out to find Joe Rockwater. And, with any luck, Delilah.

CHAPTER SEVEN

Nicky passed through Wahoe Bay, noting the rows of colorful wooden houses with their white picket fences, the whitewashed shops and the palm trees standing tall in the bright blue sky. Ken was quiet in the passenger seat beside her as she navigated her way through the residential area, looking for Joe Rockwater's house.

It was hard to picture evil lurking on these streets. They were gorgeous, alive with island life, and it was nice to see locals and their families, rather than just tourists. Still, a foreboding feeling grew in Nicky as she drove closer to the address.

Somewhere here, Delilah could be being held hostage. Or worse.

Nicky couldn't afford to lose another girl on that list. The guilt of not being able to save them all so far weighed her down every day, and it was getting harder to sleep at night. Especially after hearing Delilah's pleading voice on the recording, Nicky knew she wouldn't be able to take it if Delilah was dead.

As an FBI agent, she knew losses were sometimes unavoidable, but she had to believe that this one could be avoided if she just hurried.

When she'd been given the task of spearheading a task force designed specifically to find ten missing women, it was after Nicky had failed to save Senator Amara Gregory's daughter.

Masie Gregory had been killed only moments before Nicky had arrived, and that day still haunted her. Nicky had been doing her best to save all the missing women, but it seemed like no matter what she did, she was always one step behind. She had managed to save some of them, but it wasn't enough. The guilt of not being able to save them all gnawed at her every thought.

Nicky knew that Delilah could be facing the same fate if she didn't act quickly, and the fear drove her forward. There was no time to doubt herself. No--she had to keep believing it wasn't too late.

"You good, Lyons?" Ken asked, and Nicky glanced at him as she drove.

"I'm okay. Just thinking about the ones we've lost."

Ken nodded, looking away. "I think about them too. But it's not gonna be like that this time."

Nicky smiled, grateful for Ken's quiet support. It was nice to have someone who understood what she was going through, and it gave her the strength to keep going. Nicky had never bonded with a partner the way she had with Ken, and she hoped, once this was all over, that they could explore the romantic part of their relationship more.

Nicky didn't know what a healthy relationship looked like. She'd never been in one, and her parents' relationship had been anything but a good example. Her mother had been quiet and obedient; her father had been an alcoholic who mostly sat on the couch with a beer. And even before the kidnapping, their family dynamic had been broken.

But Nicky had to believe that it could be different. That she could find love and happiness in a relationship, just like other people did. She wanted to have a family of her own one day, to have the kind of life that she'd always dreamed of--a home filled with laughter and love. A family with love and security and support, the kind of family she'd never had before.

But that was far off down the line. If Nicky could just save Delilah, maybe she'd be able to finally find some peace. Her thoughts drifted back to her family as she drove, wondering what it would have been like if things had been different. If her parents had loved each other, and if they had shown love for their children.

Maybe then she wouldn't feel so alone all the time. Maybe then she wouldn't feel so lost in her own life. Having Ken by her side was the closest she'd ever felt to security. Even if they hadn't even kissed yet, their bond of trust had only grown stronger since they'd confessed their feelings to each other.

They could take the romance slow. And Nicky appreciated that more than Ken knew. It felt good to have someone on her side--who cared about this job as much as she did.

Ken didn't want to lose another girl as much as Nicky did.

At long last, she reached the address the bartender had given her--Joe Rockwater's house.

Nicky pulled the rental car up to a small house tucked away in a quiet neighborhood. The house was painted bright yellow and had a broad, open-air porch, giving it a charming appeal--nice-looking, for a place that might have a woman held hostage inside.

Nicky parked the car across the street and took a breath. Beside her, Ken wore a stern expression.

"You really think this guy could have Delilah?" he asked.

With sweaty palms, Nicky looked on at the house. She hoped Joe did have Delilah. She looked at the house and imagined the girl alive, behind the walls somewhere, waiting for Nicky to save her. But they wouldn't know unless they got in there.

"I hope so," Nicky muttered. "Let's go."

Without another word, they got out of the car and made their way across the street. Nicky heard music coming from Joe's backyard--a lively, upbeat tune that made her stomach twist. It was a familiar melody, like the one in the background of the recording. That awful recording of Delilah's voice, pleading for help...

Nicky shook away her nerves. They were here now, and they had to confront this guy.

She and Ken made their way around the house, through the side gate, and into Joe's backyard. There was a small group of people gathered around a daytime fire pit, drinking beer and laughing. Joe stood at the center of it all, playing guitar and singing along to his own song. He looked up as Nicky and Ken stepped into the backyard.

Joe stopped playing and put down his guitar, looking them up and down with suspicion in his eyes. The other partygoers stared back at them in silence, clearly wondering who these two strangers were.

"Are you two here for the live music?" Joe asked, his voice hesitant. "Never seen you around before..."

Nicky kept her gaze firm on him. "Joe Rockwater?"

"Yeah?" he said.

"Can we talk in private?"

The other partygoers watched apprehensively.

Joe raised an eyebrow at them. "What do you want to talk about?"

"It's about Delilah," Nicky said, her voice quiet.

At the mention of the girl's name, Joe tensed up. He glanced around at his guests, then back at Nicky and Ken. "I don't know what you're talking about," he said coolly.

Nicky felt a wave of anger wash over her. "Please, Mr. Rockwater. We need to talk in private." She subtly flashed her FBI badge.

Joe's brow furrowed as he looked from Nicky to Ken, and then back again. He hesitated for a moment, before finally nodding in agreement.

"Alright," he said. "Let's go inside."

Nicky and Ken followed Joe into his house, with the partygoers still watching them intently. Nicky kept her eyes on Joe as they walked, feeling the tension in the air as they made their way into a back room of his home. The room was filled with larger and smaller items of paraphernalia related to marijuana. There were grinders, bongs, pipes, rolling papers, lighters, and other items. Some of the items were shaped like animals or cleverly decorated with intricate designs or colorful paint jobs. A bad look, but they weren't here to be the drug police.

"So what do you want?" he asked cautiously.

Nicky took a deep breath before she answered him. She had rehearsed this conversation in her head a million times, but it still felt strange to be speaking these words out loud now that she was actually here.

"We're looking for Delilah," she said firmly. "We believe you know where she is."

Joe's face hardened at the mention of Delilah's name, and he crossed his arms over his chest defensively. "I don't know who you're talking about," he said gruffly.

Nicky could see right through him--he was hiding something--and so she pressed forward with her questions despite his resistance. "Are you sure you don't know anyone named Delilah?" she asked.

"I'm positive," Joe said. "Who the hell is she?"

Nicky took out her phone and brought up a photo of Delilah, flashing it in Joe's face. He stared at the photo, then glanced back at Nicky and Ken.

"Still sure you don't know her?" Ken asked.

"Yeah, man," Joe said. "I don't know her."

Nicky and Ken exchanged a look. They both knew he was lying, but they didn't have any evidence to prove it. Joe seemed to sense their suspicion and he stepped forward, his voice becoming stern.

"Look," he said firmly. "I don't know who this girl is or what you two are trying to find out, but I can guarantee you one thing: I don't know Delilah." He straightened up and crossed his arms over his chest again as if daring them to challenge him further.

Nicky was happy to oblige. She took out her phone, bringing up what could be their smoking gun.

The recording.

She pressed play on the first recording--the natural sound of Delilah's voice, before the background music was isolated.

"P-please... I don't know where I am... he... he said I have to talk... oh God, I'm so scared. Please, you have to come help me."

Joe frowned at them, but his expression showed he was clearly disturbed. "What is this?"

Nicky turned off the recording. "Do you recognize her voice?"

Joe shook his head adamantly. "No, I don't." He said it with such conviction that Nicky almost believed him. Almost.

But she couldn't shake the feeling that he was hiding something.

Nicky and Ken exchanged another look, then Nicky cleared her throat. "We believe she's been kidnapped," she said quietly.

Joe's face paled and he stepped back, shaking his head again in disbelief. "No... no way," he said. "That doesn't make any sense." He paused for a moment, before finally meeting their eyes again with a determined look on his face. "I don't know this Delilah person, okay? I've never seen her or heard of her before now."

He seemed sincere in his words--or at least as sincere as someone could be when they were lying through their teeth--and Nicky couldn't help but feel a bit of sympathy for him despite the fact that he was clearly trying to hide something from them.

But that wasn't the part of the recording she really wanted him to hear.

Nicky changed to the next recording, the one that had been isolated so only the background music played.

She turned it on, and the song filled the room. The twangy ukulele, plus Joe's lyrics:

"My girl went away from me...

She was lost...

Lost at sea...

My girl was gone...

She had no choice...

She lost her voice..."

Nicky turned off the recording and looked at Joe, who had eyes full of tears. The sad look on his face caught her off guard, and she exchanged a confused look with Ken. Was Joe crumbling under the pressure? Maybe he suddenly realized the weight of what he'd done to Delilah... maybe he was finally feeling guilt.

But then he said, "That song... I wrote it for my girlfriend... I haven't heard it in so long."

"Your girlfriend?" Nicky asked, raising an eyebrow.

Joe snapped from his daze, meeting Nicky's eyes. "My girlfriend, Amelia. She got lost at sea many years ago, and I wrote that song when I was in my late twenties for her. It's on my debut album. I... I haven't played it in a long time."

Nicky and Ken looked at each other, not sure what to make of this story. Was Joe telling the truth? Or was it just a clever ploy to distract them from their investigation?

Joe looked away from them, and Nicky saw that his hands were trembling. He was clearly shaken up, but he still hadn't given them the answers they needed.

"Do you know what happened to Delilah?" she asked, her voice gentle.

Joe shook his head slowly. "I don't... I mean, I don't know who she is. I swear I don't."

"This is a fairly obscure song," Nicky noted. "Any massive fans of your work you know of?"

"Well, no," Joe rambled, "but--"

"Then you have to admit this is a strange coincidence," Ken cut in. "Maybe we should take a look around at your house."

Joe stiffened. "You can't do that," he said.

Nicky straightened up. So, he was putting up a fight. That didn't look good.

Maybe Delilah was even in here.

"Really?" Nicky said. "If you have nothing to hide, it shouldn't be a problem."

Joe shook his head resolutely. "I don't want you snooping around in my house. I don't know what happened to Delilah, and I don't want you to think I'm hiding something. I just don't want you to invade my privacy."

"A woman's life is on the line here," Nicky said. "Forgive us if we're not overly concerned about your belongings. We only want Delilah."

"Well, I don't have her!" Joe exclaimed.

"Then we should be able to look around, no problem," Ken said.

Joe's fists clenched, and he took a step forward. Nicky saw a flash of anger in his eyes, and she knew they had pushed him too far.

Before either of them could react, Joe lunged right at Ken.

CHAPTER EIGHT

Nicky pulled her gun out and trained it right on Joe.

Joe pushed Ken back against the wall, and Ken's eyes widened in shock.

"Don't you dare come into my house," Joe growled. "You don't know what you're talking about. I don't know where Delilah is, and I'm not going to let you come in here and accuse me of something I didn't do."

Nickie stepped forward, her gun right on him. "Joe, calm down," she said. The man was unarmed, and Nicky doubted he could do much damage to a seasoned agent like Ken without a weapon--but she wasn't about to take any risks.

Joe didn't seem to realize the gun was even on him. He kept his eyes on Ken, glowering like a rabid animal. Ken glared back, unfazed, unafraid.

"Joe," Nicky warned again. "Unhand Agent Walker. Now."

Joe hesitated, then slowly stepped back, his hands in the air.

"That's it," Nicky said. "Now, Nicky, cuff him."

Nicky moved in quickly, her gun still trained on Joe as she pulled out her handcuffs. She cuffed him, and then stepped back, her gun still ready. Ken dusted himself off as he stepped away from Joe, still remaining stoic.

"That wasn't very smart of you, Mr. Rockwater," Ken said.

Once Joe was securely cuffed, Nicky patted him down to make sure he wasn't carrying any weapons. She found nothing, and she stepped back to survey her handiwork. Joe was now securely restrained, and the look of anger in his eyes had been replaced with resignation.

Nicky sighed. This was not the way she had wanted the investigation to go, but it was the way it had ended up. She looked up at Ken and saw a look of understanding in his eyes. He knew that sometimes, you had to take extreme measures in order to get the job done.

"Wait here with him," Nicky instructed Ken, "and call the local PD. I'll take a look around."

Nicky gestured to the house. This time, Joe didn't resist. It seemed he'd accepted his fate.

Nicky stepped into the house, her gun in hand, her eyes scanning the room for any signs of Delilah. She had no idea what she was looking for, but she was determined to find something. She searched the living room first, her gaze lingering on any object that could possibly hide something. The living room was littered with marijuana pipes, bongs, and rolling papers, along with several guitars and amps. Scattered amongst them were musical scores and books on musical theory. The scent that filled the room was a mix of musky marijuana smoke and sweet-smelling incense.

She moved to the kitchen next, overwhelmed by the smell of rotting food in the sink. The kitchen was a mess. Dirty dishes and rotting food littered the counters and floors. A large pile of garbage filled one corner, overflowing with things that should have been thrown out long ago. Flies buzzed around aimlessly, drawn to the decaying remains of something once edible. The taste was bitter and acidic, like old milk or spoiled fish left out for too long. It was a taste that Nicky was all too familiar with, a reminder of the consequences of neglect. She'd been in many homes in worse shape than this--it seemed more like Joe was too lazy to clean up after himself.

Still nothing that indicated his guilt.

But as she made her way to the back of the house, she noticed something odd. The door to the basement was slightly ajar, and Nicky could feel a chill coming from it. She stepped closer, peering down into the darkness. Something about it made her uneasy, but she knew she had to investigate.

Nicky slowly descended the stairs, her gun still at the ready. As she reached the bottom, she felt a wave of cold air coming from the darkness. She could see nothing, but she felt like she was being watched. She took a deep breath and stepped forward, her heart pounding in her chest. She could hear a noise getting louder as she got closer. It was a soft whimpering, and she was hit with a bad smell--like wet dog--as she reached the bottom floor.

Nicky felt around for a light and flicked it on.

Then, all of a sudden, the sound of barking drilled her from all angles.

Nicky gasped as she saw the basement was filled with cages, each containing a different dog. It was a heartbreaking sight. The dogs were all thin and malnourished, their fur matted and dull... until Nicky took a closer look, and realized that many of these dogs were Nicky of a much higher quality than what she had initially realized. Their fur was soft and glossy, and their coats were bright and full. It was clear to Nicky that these animals had been neglected and abused, but despite this, they still seemed to be of a rare or expensive breed. What was this, some kind of underground dog black market? Nicky had no idea, but she didn't like it.

Still, she was looking for a missing woman--a human--not a dog.

Nicky searched the basement, but there was no sign of Delilah anywhere. All she found were the dogs, and a deep sense of sadness that lingered in the air.

That didn't mean Joe was innocent. He was clearly guilty of holding these likely-stolen animals--so maybe he had Delilah somewhere else.

Either way, they had a solid case here. Joe wouldn't get away with this--whatever "this" was.

***

Nicky stood in Joe Rockwater's living room as the police escorted him outside. More officers were downstairs, concocting their plan to safely remove all of the dogs and return them either to shelters, or to their owners.

No sign of Delilah had been found anywhere in the house, but Nicky wasn't done with Joe by a longshot.

An officer came up to her and said, "Agent Lyons, thank you."

Nicky turned to see a young man with dark hair and kind eyes.

"Someone has been stealing tourists' dogs for some time," the officer explained. "You probably didn't hear about it, as it might be a bit below your pay grade, but it's something we've been racking our brains over. I think you cracked the case here."

"What do you think he's doing with them?" Nicky asked. "Selling them? They were clearly treated poorly."

"We'll find out," the officer assured.

"Good." Nicky nodded. "And I need your men to search any other properties Joe Rockwater might have access to."

"We'll try, but Joe doesn't have very much money," the officer said. "He doesn't own any other properties. We suspect he is selling and stealing the dogs just to get an extra dollar."

Nicky sighed. She was worried about Delilah. If Joe wasn't holding her anywhere else, then where was she? She had to be somewhere--but where?

Nicky looked out the window, where Joe was being put into the back of a police car. Nicky made a snap choice--she needed to talk to him again. She rushed out the front door and to the street, stopping outside the car.

"Joe," she said.

The police officer holding him stepped aside so Nicky could talk to him.

"What do you want?" Joe said. "You've already ruined me."

"Where is Delilah?" Nicky pressed, her throat tight.

"I told you, I don't know who the hell that is," Joe insisted.

Nicky stared at him for a moment, searching for any sign of guilt or fear in his eyes. But there was nothing. He seemed genuinely confused and unaware.

Maybe he really didn't know. Maybe he was innocent. Nicky sighed, feeling a wave of frustration. She had been so sure that Joe was the key to finding Delilah, but now she wasn't so sure. All she had were a bunch of dogs and a mystery.

"You really don't know?" Nicky asked.

"I have nothing else to lose," Joe said. "I have nothing else to hide. Whoever this woman is, she isn't with me."

Nicky nodded. She didn't want to think that Joe was innocent, but it seemed like he might be telling the truth. Still, she couldn't shake the feeling that there was more to the story. Even then, Joe wasn't going anywhere; if he did have Delilah, they would know soon enough. But if he didn't, then Nicky couldn't waste more time on him. Someone had Delilah.

She had to keep looking, no matter how impossible it seemed.

CHAPTER NINE

As it turned out, having one was better than two.

The man paced across his basement, his head hurting from the noise. Too much noise. Too many voices to choose from--how had he even considered a third?

No, he had two women--but he only needed one.

One to love, one to be with, one to make his heart beat faster. One who he could trust and rely on, and who would be there for him no matter what life threw his way.

He had chosen well. In the end, it was better to have one strong, loyal partner than to have two different people in his life whom he had to constantly juggle and compete for his attention. One to sing to him and fill his ears with her lovely voice.

One was enough. But he had made to make right decision.

The two women were tied up in the chairs, beside each other now, whimpers coming from them as they sat with their heads low, their limbs still bound by the ropes he'd carefully wrapped around them.

He needed to hear them again. One-by-one.

So, he tapped Delilah on the head. She looked up at him with teary eyes. "W-what?"

He nodded at her, then gestured his finger to his mouth. He pointed up. She had been with him for a long time now, and she often knew what he meant.

"You want me to sing again?" she asked, her voice weak.

Beside her, the other woman--June, as it turned out was her name--said, "Will this freak ever let us go?"

Delilah looked at her and shook her head. But she was wrong. He would let one of them go.

In death, only.

He tapped Delilah again, and gestured for her to sing.

She nodded, and closed her eyes.

And the man sat back and listened as she sang, her voice trembling but still strong, as if it knew that it could be her last song.

It was good enough. He'd gotten used to Delilah's voice in the several months he'd had her with him, and it had almost grown stale.

That was what had prompted him to go out and find another. June had been busking on the street, and she had a surprisingly lovely voice, considering she was also known to be a sex worker.

But could she be good enough to replace Delilah, permanently? He still wasn't sure.

He gestured for June to sing now, and she did, her voice quivering with fear but still strong enough.

The man compared the two voices, one after the other. He wanted to make sure he made the right decision--the one that would keep him happy for a long time to come.

And so, he made Delilah and June compete with their singing, judging them on pitch, tone, and emotion.

Delilah's was powerful and well-practiced, while June's was fresh and raw. It was almost like they were two different kinds of music--one soothing and familiar, the other exciting and new.

He'd have to decide which one he wanted soon...

But it was too hard! He couldn't make up his mind!

Suddenly, he had an idea. He would let them decide for themselves. He held up his hand, signaling for them to stop, and they did. They needed to make up his mind for him, but how? A game, perhaps. Yes... a game.

He held out his fist and then slapped it against his open hand. Then, made a scissoring gesture with his fingers.

The women glanced at each other, perplexed.

"What the hell is this?" June said.

"Rock paper scissors?" Delilah asked timidly. "You want us to play?"

Delilah! She was so smart, and so faithful. Part of him was now hoping she'd win.

He nodded with a wide smile.

June groaned. "This is ridiculous! Let us go already!"

But the man shook his head and gestured for them to start playing.

June shook her head. "No way! I'm not playing this game with you. Let me go." She tried to stand up, but the ropes were still binding her to the chair.

He frowned and grabbed a knife from his pocket, pointing it at June menacingly. She glowered at him, then relaxed in the chair.

"Just do whatever he says," Delilah told her. "It's the only way."

"He won't even say anything!" June shouted, her voice grating.

His hair stood on end. He didn't like that tone. He needed a good voice, a voice to speak and sing for him.

He wondered if that FBI agent had received his clues yet. He'd paid a lot of money to sneak a cassette into her mailbox, and paid even more to get her personal information. The FBI agent he'd seen on the news... he'd first heard about her when the vice president's daughters went missing, and had been following traces of her career since.

Nicky Lyons.

She was the type of person who had a voice. Who people listened to.

And as he'd followed what snippets he could get of her career on the news, he'd discovered her job was dedicated to finding missing girls.

She would listen to him.

He knew it.

But it was true--he didn't need two voices, only one.

That was enough. A choice had to be made.

He pointed the knife at them, firmer this time, demanding that they play.

Delilah and June looked at each other nervously. They didn't want to do this, but they had no choice.

They began to play rock paper scissors, their hands shaking as they threw out their symbols. The man watched them intently, his jaw clenched tight as he waited for the results.

Whoever emerged victorious would live.

The loser would die.

Then, he would finally be heard.

CHAPTER TEN

Nicky focused on the road ahead as she and Ken drove through Wahoe Bay, headed toward the police station, because truthfully, Nicky didn't know where else to go.

Joe Rockwater had been their lead, but it looked like he was innocent--at least of kidnapping humans. The police had scoured Joe's house and the homes of his known friends and associates, but there was no sign of Delilah anywhere. They were here in the Bahamas, and yet they were no closer to finding out the truth about Delilah.

Nicky's next best guess was that the kidnapper had one of Joe's CDs, and since Joe was local, it seemed likely the killer could still be in Wahoe Bay. So at least they were potentially on the right track.

But still, Nicky couldn't help but feel anxious that they were nowhere near where Delilah was, and all of this was a ruse. She focused on the road, but her mind was swimming.

Just then, Ken's voice broke into her thoughts.

"Hey, I was just thinking about something."

Nicky glanced over at him, her eyebrows raising in surprise. "What is it?"

"Well, I was thinking about the cassette tape the kidnapper sent you. We're a long way from Jacksonville. Do you think he even delivered it himself?"

Nicky's heart began to race. That was a good point. If the kidnapper was here in Wahoe Bay, then he probably didn't deliver the tape himself. They hadn't received an update from Grace, and it wasn't like her to not check in.

"We should call Grace and see if they have any updates," Nicky said. "Can you ring her and put it on speaker?"

Ken did as Nicky asked, dialing Grace and putting it on speaker so they could both talk to her while Nicky drove. Within a few rings, Grace picked up.

"Ken," she breathed out, "I was just about to call you two. Things are a mess over here."

Nicky exchanged a frown with Ken.

"A mess how, Grace?" Nicky asked.

"Oh, good!" Grace exclaimed through the phone. "Nicky, I'm glad you're there too. Look, you guys, we have no footage from the mail room and Nicky's apartment."

Nicky's stomach dropped. Damn. So much for that lead.

"So what's the big mess?" Ken asked.

Grace sighed. "Okay, look... the chief wanted to keep this in so you two can focus on the case, but the truth is, we're really baffled that someone was able to breach your data, Nicky. It shouldn't have happened, and we're kicking ourselves over here trying to figure out how it happened."

Nicky gritted her teeth, feeling the anger and frustration boiling inside of her. Whoever had sent her that tape had violated her privacy in many ways, and it disturbed her that she didn't have a face to attach this to.

"Can you give us any leads on who might have done it?" Nicky asked Grace, her voice low and controlled.

Grace hesitated on the other end of the line. "I can't say for sure, unfortunately. That's why things are so messy. The chief is up in arms. We're doing the best we can."

Nicky exchanged a look with Ken. "We need to know who these individuals are, Grace. The more information we have, the better chance we have of finding Delilah."

"I know," Grace said. "I'll email you both the information we have so far. But please, be careful. We don't know who we can trust at this point."

Nicky thanked Grace before hanging up the phone, her mind racing with thoughts and ideas. They needed to find Delilah, and fast. But with every lead they followed, it seemed like they were only getting further away from the truth. She glanced over at Ken, who was staring out the window, lost in thought.

"Any ideas?" she asked him.

Ken shook his head. "Not really. But we need to keep pushing forward. We'll find her, Nicky. We just need to keep trying until something sticks."

Nicky nodded, thinking back to the mail room. "Maybe the kidnapper didn't deliver the package himself," Nicky said, "or maybe he did, and he's nowhere near here."

Her mind was spinning with possibilities. But one thing was for sure—they needed to find out the answer to this question.

And fast.

As Nicky was driving, her phone buzzed in the console of the rental car. Her heart jumped--maybe it was an update from the prison. She nodded at Ken.

"Can you check that? It might be the CI I told you about."

Ken opened up her phone as she drove along the roadside beach. The police station was somewhere up the shore.

"It's..." Ken frowned. "It's an attachment from an unknown number."

Nicky's stomach dropped. "What?"

"It's an audio recording."

Nicky pulled over to the side of the road and took a deep breath. An audio recording. Could it be...

She looked back at Ken, her heart racing. Outside of the car, the beach stretched on endlessly, and the sea continued into the horizon. Surely, it couldn't be from the kidnapper. He'd already sent the cassette tape. Why would he need to do that if he had her phone number?

It didn't matter. She needed to know.

"Play it," she told Ken.

He did.

A calm whooshing filled the car, and it wasn't from the beach outside.

It was coming from the phone.

They heard faint crying in the recording, along with the sound of water. Nicky's heart skipped a beat. Could it be? Was this Delilah? Were they getting closer to finding her?

Nicky grabbed the phone from Ken and put it to her ear, straining to hear over the noise of the waves outside. She could just make out a voice in the background—it sounded like a man's voice, but she couldn't tell what was being said.

The recording abruptly ended and Nicky pulled away from the phone, her heart pounding in her chest. She looked at Ken, who seemed just as startled as she was.

But that crying...

It could be Delilah's.

Delilah was almost certainly still alive. The relief that flooded through Nicky was like a wave crashing over her, washing away all of her fear and doubt.

It had to be the kidnapper who sent this—he must have been nearby and wanted them to know that they were on the right track. The sound of the beach could easily be here. The clue about Joe Rockwater's music--the kidnapper must have wanted them to follow it here. And now he was sending another breadcrumb.

But just because there was crying in the recording didn't mean Delilah would be alive for long.

No, she could still die. All of this felt like a cruel, twisted game.

Like he was punishing Delilah as a way to punish Nicky.

The thought was too much for Nicky, and the panic began to well up inside her. Her hands shook as she tried to steady her breathing. She felt like she was going to have a panic attack right there in the car.

Ken must have noticed because he reached out and put his hand on her shoulder, trying to calm her down.

"Hey, Nicky, it's gonna be okay," he said. "We've dealt with shit like this before. We'll figure it out."

"Why is he fixating on me?" Nicky asked. "What if he hurts her to send some sort of message to me?"

"He might be keeping her alive to send a message to you," Ken countered. "We don't know anything. We can't make assumptions."

He paused for a moment, and Nicky could feel his gaze on her.

"But," he continued, "we can look for clues. We can get to the bottom of this." He pointed out the window at the beach, which stretched on forever into the horizon. "We're close, now. We just need to keep going, and we'll find Delilah."

Nicky nodded slowly and took a deep breath, trying to push back her fear. She knew Ken was right—they had come too far to give up now. They just needed to stay focused and take it one step at a time.

She looked out at the beach again, feeling calmer as she watched the waves crash against the shoreline in an endless rhythm. She thought of the lake house all those years ago, when she was last with Rosie, her sister... how the water had always both somehow calmed her and reminded her of the worst experience of her life.

Maybe Delilah was going through what Nicky and Rosie had gone through. Maybe it was even worse.

After all, Nicky had only been held captive in that lake house for three days before she'd escaped. Rosie had been left behind, of course, and stayed with the kidnapper... presumably forever, if she was even still alive.

Nicky wondered what the man had done to her sister.

Had he kept her alive? Or had he killed her soon after Nicky escaped?

The thought made Nicky's chest tighten. She wanted to believe that Rosie was still alive—that she had somehow managed to survive all these years, despite the odds. But it was hard to stay hopeful when so much time had passed without any news of her sister.

Still, Nicky felt a strange comfort in being here at the beach—a reminder of the bond between her and Rosie that could never be broken.

She looked out at the horizon and imagined Rosie standing there beside her, watching the waves crash against the shoreline like they used to do when they were kids, only they had been looking at lakes in West Virginia, not the beautiful beaches of the Bahamas.

If Delilah could be found alive, maybe Rosie could too.

Nicky couldn't help but feel parallels between this case and her sister's. Both young girls, both named after flowers...

But she had no reason to think this could be connected. Felix had slipped to Garrison that Rosie's kidnapper was still somewhere in West Virginia, not here in Wahoe Bay. And besides, the MO didn't line up.

Rosie's kidnapper had a thing for sisters.

But Delilah was an only child. And she was taken alone.

Still, Nicky couldn't help the feeling that this was somehow related.

But if it was, she had no idea how.

She took a deep breath and tried to shake off her thoughts. Right now, she had to focus on Delilah. She had to find her and bring her home. Nicky felt her panic begin to relax as she took in all of the scenery around them—the sun slid across midday sky, and the ocean was crystal clear.

She had to ground herself and think of the next steps. They needed to send this audio to forensics back at the FBI HQ in Jacksonville and see if they could trace any part of it. The number it came from. Anything.

"Okay," Nicky breathed out, "we need to see what forensics can do with this audio. And then, we need to explore the area. See if we can find any clues or evidence that might help us locate Delilah."

Ken nodded in agreement, and Nicky felt her confidence start to grow. She was determined to get Delilah back—no matter what it took. She took her phone and forwarded the message and audio file to Grace's email, then quickly called Grace's number. Within moments, the tech answered:

"Nicky--"

"Grace, I just sent you a file and a message I got to my phone," Nicky said. She stared out the windshield of the car, at the bay extending before them. "I think it's the kidnapper. We need the audio analyzed, and see if you can get a trace on where the message came from."

"On it, Nicky," Grace said, then added, "We're working on the 'how' this guy is sending all this stuff to you, but what's bothering me more is: why?"

"I wish I knew, Grace," Nicky said. "But something tells me if we don't act fast, this could get a lot uglier."

Grace was quiet for a moment, and then said, "I'm on it. I'm already running a trace. I'll get back to you as soon as I have something."

"Thanks, Grace," Nicky said, and hung up.

Nicky looked at Ken and gave him a determined nod.

"Let's go. We still have work to do."

CHAPTER ELEVEN

"One room, please," Nicky said to the hotel clerk, who looked up at her with a smile. The young girl, a Bahamas native, glanced behind Nicky and looked at Ken.

"One bed or two?" she asked.

Nicky's chest burned, and she glanced at Ken to see he was looking off at the hotel lobby. He casually shrugged as he looked at her and said, "One's fine with me if it is with you."

Nicky swallowed hard, but nodded and turned to the clerk. "Let's go with one."

Forensics still hadn't gotten back to them, but Nicky knew they would soon--until then, they needed a quiet place to think and work, so they decided to check into a hotel early. It was just barely the afternoon, so they wouldn't be sleeping any time soon, but Nicky was still nervous. She had Ken had accelerated their relationship beyond simple FBI partners--they were into each other, that much was clear. They had each other's backs.

But they hadn't kissed, and they certainly hadn't thought about sharing a bed like that.

Then again, maybe it was time. If they ended up having to stay overnight here, then Nicky knew she'd be racked awake by anxiety about finding Delilah--and having Ken's warmth beside her would help.

There was no pressure to push it further.

"One is fine," Nicky told the clerk.

The clerk nodded and handed Nicky a keycard. "Your room is on the second floor, just down the hall."

Nicky thanked her and took the keycard. She looked at Ken, who was still looking away, then smiled to herself and headed in the direction of the stairs. She felt his presence behind her as they walked up to their room. The hotel was nice--obviously geared toward tourists who wanted to stay in the main area of town, rather than on a resort. The décor had a charm only known to the Bahamas. When they reached their room, she inserted the card into the door handle. With a soft click, the lock opened.

The décor of the room had an old-fashioned Caribbean style, with most of the furnishings crafted from mahogany that was a dark brownish color, not the yellowish hue seen on many older pieces. The wicker furniture was big and bulky, with cushions the size of pillows. The bed linens were some type of cotton print in turquoise and green stripes.

Nicky felt relieved as she looked around--it was exactly what they needed for now. She glanced at Ken, who still hadn't said anything about sharing one bed or not. But he seemed just as relieved as she did to have somewhere quiet to work for now. Not that they had much to go on--not until forensics got back to them, but Nicky anticipated they'd get word any minute.

Nicky sat down on the bed. It was stiff, but good enough. Ken sat beside her, a fair distance away, but she felt his weight beside her.

"So..." He rubbed the back of his neck. "You're really okay with us sharing a bed?"

Embarrassment flooded her, so she deflected with a lighthearted, "Who says we're sharing a bed? You can take the floor."

Ken chuckled, but his face was read. "Maybe I can crash in the bathtub instead."

They both laughed, but it was followed by a tense silence. Nicky glanced over at Ken to see his intense blue eyes on hers.

"For real, Nicky," he said. "We can still take things slow. I know you have a lot on your mind, not just with this case, but with your sister."

Nick nodded. "I know," she said softly.

"We can take it one step at a time," he said. "I'm here for you, no matter what."

Nicky felt the warmth of his words spread through her like wildfire. She took his hand and gave it a light squeeze.

"Thank you," she said. "For understanding."

Ken nodded, a small smile on his lips. He leaned in and brushed his lips against her cheek, a sweet, gentle kiss that left her feeling like she was floating. It was just a kiss on the cheek, but it made her feel like she wanted to be ten times closer to him--like this whole "taking it slow" thing was a bunch of bullshit.

Nicky had never taken anything slow when it came to relationships--more so, she had started them quickly and ended them just as fast. But this thing with Ken felt real, and she didn't want to mess it up.

So she pulled away before her desire got the best of her, and stood up.

"Let's get to work," she said, trying to sound more sure of herself than she felt.

Ken gave her a knowing look, but nodded. They went and set up their laptops on the small table across from the bed.

Just as they were getting settled, Nicky's phone rang. She answered without looking at the caller ID--and heard the familiar voice of Grace.

"Hey, Nicky," she said. "We've analyzed the recording. I'm sending it to you now. As for the trace, well..."

Nicky waited with bated breath for Grace to continue.

"Well, we couldn't trace where it's from," Grace said. "It's a fake phone number using an encrypted app."

Nicky sighed, her shoulders sagging. "Damn."

"But we did find something else," Grace said. "We think the kidnapper is using a specific type of microphone, so we're looking into what it could be."

"That's a start," Nicky said. "Where do we start looking?"

"We're already on it," Grace said. "We're doing some digging, and we'll get back to you as soon as we have something. Until then, I've sent a few audio files--we isolated the voice in the background of the call. I think you should listen to it."

Nicky nodded, determined. "Will do. Thanks, Grace."

With that, she hung up.

She took a deep breath, then turned to Ken.

"Ready?" she asked.

He nodded, his expression determined. "Let's do this."

Nicky opened her laptop and clicked on the audio file Grace sent over. She hit play, and they both leaned in as the recording began to play. They could hear a man's voice; even isolated, it was difficult to make out his words, but he had a strong, stern cadence, almost like a man doing a speech. Like with Joe's music, it sounded like it was happening in the background, not the focal point of the call.

Nicky and Ken listened intently, trying to make out the words and any other clues they could get. Finally, there was a pause in the recording, and the man's voice became clearer.

"You know what you have to do," he said. "We have a plan, and it must be executed to the letter. No mistakes, no deviations. We have to be successful, for all our sakes. Failure is not an option."

Then, what followed sounded like cheers and clapping from a crowd.

The voice trailed off, and the recording ended.

Nicky and Ken looked at each other in shock. Was it just her, or did that sound like some sort of rally?

The way the man spoke--he almost had the cadence of a politician of some kind.

Nicky looked at Ken, her mind spinning. "I think we should check out any political rallies in the area." That way, they might be able to identify the man's voice, and hopefully find a lead.

Ken nodded. "Good idea. Let's get to work."

They started to research on their laptops, looking for any political rallies that had been held in the area recently. It turned out that Wahoe Bay was having an election for their new mayor. Nicky opened up a few news articles and scanned through them, while Ken searched for any social media posts about rallies or protests that had happened recently. As they worked, Nicky felt her heart racing with excitement--maybe this would be the break they needed.

"What about this one?" Ken offered, turning his computer toward Nicky. It showed an article about a man who was running for mayor against the current mayor, who was up for re-election. He'd held a rally yesterday at a library downtown.

Nicky thought on it. That could be good, but then again, the voice wasn't all they'd heard in the recording. Aside from the crying, there had also been...

The ocean.

"No," Nicky said, "I think we're looking at something that happened by the shore."

Ken nodded. "So, what about this one?" He pointed to another article about a protest that had been held two weeks ago by the beach. Nicky read through it quickly; it was a peaceful demonstration against the proposed construction of a new resort, which many locals were opposed to. Henry Minns, the current mayor of Wahoe Bay, had shown up in support and to also campaign his re-election.

But it had happened two weeks ago.

"We're probably looking for something more recent," Nicky said.

"Let's keep looking, then," Ken said eagerly. "Maybe we can find out more about this guy."

Nicky smiled and nodded; they were onto something here. She kept searching online, combing through articles and posts related to the rally and its attendees, looking for any clues or hints that might point them in the right direction.

Then, Nicky came across Henry's social media page.

He had posted about a rally by the shore.

A rally that was happening today, at eleven a.m.

Nicky checked the time. It was after noon, but the rally could still be going on.

Her heart raced.

It could even be the same rally the recording had been taken at.

"Ken, I think we have something," Nicky said, her voice filled with excitement. She showed him the post on Henry's page.

"Shit, he could be there now," Ken said. "Do we think Henry could be a suspect?"

"I doubt it," Nicky said. "I think someone there took the recording. But I think, like with Joe's music, they want us to hear it. Or, they want *me* to hear it."

She paused, her thoughts racing. "We need to get to the rally. Now."

Ken nodded, and they quickly gathered their things and left the hotel, heading straight for the beach.

No matter what they found there, Nicky just hoped it would lead them closer to Delilah, before it was too late.

CHAPTER TWELVE

Nicky hurried toward the beachside rally with Ken at her side, sweat forming on her brown from the hot afternoon sun. As they arrived, they could see a large crowd gathered on the beach, listening to a man on a podium. Nicky's heart leaped as she recognized the voice--it was Henry.

"If given the opportunity to continue as your mayor, I would never put tourism over the comfort and safety of our own people!"

Nick watched as Henry spoke, his words ringing out across the crowd. He was passionate and charismatic, and the crowd cheered him on. Nicky felt a chill run down her spine. It had to be him--the same voice from the recording.

She leaned in closer, straining to hear what he was saying.

"We must fight the corruption that has taken over our town," he said. "We must fight for what is right! Together, we can make a difference!"

The crowd erupted in cheers, and Nicky knew they were onto something. She turned to Ken, and he nodded.

As they drew closer, Nicky could feel the energy in the air; it seemed like dozens of people were gathered around the makeshift stage, listening eagerly as Henry Minns spoke passionately about his campaign promises. His words echoed off the waves, and Nicky felt her heart skip a beat--she had a feeling that this might be the rally they were looking for. It all sounded exactly like the recording did, along with the waves crashing on the shore.

Of course, there was no woman crying.

The two of them pushed through the crowd until they were close enough to get a good view of the stage. Nicky's eyes widened as she recognized Henry from his social media posts; he was definitely the man from their recording. She glanced over at Ken, who nodded in agreement; this was it.

Nicky watched Henry intently as he continued to speak, captivated by his words and charisma. He seemed to have a way with words that made it easy for him to connect with his audience--and by the looks of it, he had won them over in no time.

But they weren't looking for Henry. No, they were looking for someone else here.

Maybe even Delilah herself.

"My voice is for the people!" Henry announced, and the crowd clapped again.

Nicky and Ken scanned the crowd, searching for any sign of Delilah. But there was nothing--just a sea of faces that had come out to support Henry Minns.

But they weren't going to give up that easily; they needed to keep looking until they found something that could help lead them closer to finding Delilah. With renewed determination, Nicky and Ken made their way back through the crowd, determined to keep searching until they got the answers they were looking for. It was a longshot, but maybe someone in the crowd might recognize Delilah.

Nicky pulled up a photo and went up to the first person she saw, showing the phone to a woman. "Have you seen this girl?" Nicky asked

The woman shook her head and dismissed Nicky, saying she hadn't seen anyone like that.

Nicky sighed as she walked away, feeling a bit defeated. But she knew they had to keep looking; this was their only chance of finding Delilah before it was too late. She glanced up at the sky, feeling a gentle breeze on her face. They had to press on and find her--for Delilah's sake and for their own.

Nicky went on to the next person, repeating the process of showing the photo of Delilah. The next person, a man, shushed her before she could even get out her question, so she darted to the next. Ken was doing the same, moving through the crowd and asking people about Delilah.

"Shh, we're trying to listen!" one man said to her, and Nicky could see how into Henry's speech people were.

It was no use.

No one had seen Delilah, and if they had, they weren't giving Nicky the time of day to even think about it.

Nicky's shoulders slumped as she realized they were back to square one. She had been so sure that this rally was the answer, but it seemed like they had reached a dead end. With a heavy heart, she trudged back to Ken and met him within the crowd--they were no closer to finding Delilah than before.

They both stood in silence, feeling lost and discouraged. They had come so close, yet the answer still eluded them. It seemed like their mission was doomed before it even began.

Nicky walked off to the outskirts of the crowd, and Ken followed, his hands in the pockets of his slacks. They were overdressed for the Bahamas heat, and Nicky's clothes stuck to her back. She realized she hadn't had a glass of water in hours.

Ken sighed and looked around the crowd. "This isn't getting us anywhere. Maybe she was never hear, Lyons."

"Someone was," Nicky said. "We heard a woman crying in the recording."

"Maybe it was at another beach. Nothing seems off here."

Nicky agreed; the crowd was peaceful and friendly, but nothing seemed out of place. Still, Nicky couldn't shake the feeling in her gut that there was more to this.

"We can't give up," she told Ken. "There could be something we're missing here."

Suddenly, they heard a loud scream from the docks.

The two of them snapped their heads up in surprise and fear. What could have caused that? They looked towards the docks, and Nicky could feel her heart start to race as she realized it must be Delilah. Without another thought, they ran towards the docks. The crowd had stopped and were looking around in confusion at the scream, so Nicky and Ken darted between them, heading straight for the docks. Nicky's pulse raced faster than her feet could keep up with--that scream.

It could be her.

Delilah.

As they reached the docks, they saw a figure standing there--a woman, looking down at the water. But it was a woman Nicky had never seen before, an older lady, and Nicky's heart sank.

"Ma'am, are you okay?" Nicky asked as she and Ken charged down the docks, the sound of their feet on the wood echoing into the afternoon sky.

With a pale face, the woman pointed down at the docks.

"Look," she said, her voice trembling.

Nicky and Ken looked down at the water and saw a body floating there--a body of a woman.

For a moment, Nicky's body froze. Her worst fears flashed before her eyes.

Delilah's body, floating here, dead.

She'd failed again.

She thought of all the girls on the list so far, the ones she hadn't been able to save. She saw their faces in her dreams sometimes, along with Rosie's.

All her failures flashed before her eyes. Now, Delilah would be added to that long list of tragedies.

The people Nicky couldn't save.

It felt like the world was crashing down on her head.

The panic attack began to take hold. Nicky felt her heart racing, her palms getting sweaty, and tears streaming down her face as she collapsed onto the dock. She was shaking uncontrollably, unable to process what was happening.

She felt her throat tighten and her eyes well up with tears. Her stomach churned and she felt like she might be sick. It was too much--all the pain, all the suffering she'd seen, all the people she had failed to save. Her heart raced faster and faster as her breathing quickened. She felt a tightness in her chest, like it was being squeezed by an invisible hand. Her head spun and she felt dizzy and lightheaded.

"Lyons," Ken said, and at his voice, Nicky snapped out of it. He pointed down at the body.

As she looked closer at the body, Nicky realized that it wasn't Delilah. She felt her heart sink with relief, and yet a wave of sadness washed over her. This woman was someone's daughter, someone's sister--and here she was, dead in the water.

Her life mattered. But it wasn't Delilah's, and Nicky couldn't resist the wave of relief, as guilty as that made her feel.

But who was this woman? She had ginger hair, like Delilah, and couldn't have been much older than thirty. She was older than Delilah, and their only shared feature was their hair, so was she really connected to the case?

No, she had to be. The recording sent to Nicky's phone had come from this rally, on this shore.

And here was a woman, dead.

Was it a message?

A message that soon, the killer would kill Delilah too?

What game was he playing?

Nicky turned to the witness, who looked at them in horror. Nicky flashed her FBI badge.

"Please, ma'am, go wait over there while we get the police in here."

Nicky said softly.

The woman nodded and ran off, leaving Nicky and Ken to the body.

Nicky shook her head and turned back to the corpse, her mind whirling with questions and suspicions. Who was this woman? Was she connected to the case? Was the killer sending another message?

Nicky and Ken exchanged a look, both knowing that this was far from over.

"Who do you think she is?" Ken asked.

"I don't know," Nicky told him. "But I don't believe she's here by accident. The killer put here here. He had to."

"You really think this has to do with Delilah?" Ken asked.

"It has to," Nicky replied.

She looked back down at the body and tried to piece together what was happening. She knew the killer was trying to send a message, but what was it? What did this woman have to do with Delilah?

Nicky's thoughts were interrupted by the sound of sirens in the distance. The police were here, and Nicky and Ken had to start piecing together who this woman was--and how she fit into their case.

CHAPTER THIRTEEN

The rally had been cleared, leaving the beach open for the police to come in and do their work. Nicky stood off to the side of the docks, a queasy feeling in her stomach as she watched the Bahamas police pull the body out of the water. The woman's clothes were soaking wet, and her skin was definitely waterlogged, but the kill looked fresh.

Nicky bit down on her thumb as she watched them place the woman carefully on the dock, getting ready to transport her.

That crying voice on the recording...

It wasn't Delilah.

It was this woman.

But who was she, and how did her voice end up on Nicky's phone? She scanned the area, taking in the faces of the officers as they worked, then glanced back at the town, where the people looked on in the distance, curious about what was going on.

The witness--the woman who had found the body--stood back from the dock, speaking with Ken. Taking her eyes off the officers, Nicky went over to talk to them.

"And you saw nothing beforehand?" Ken was in the middle of asking the woman.

The woman shook her head, her eyes wide. "No, nothing. I was just standing there, looking out at the water, and then I looked over and saw the body. It was so sudden, it scared me."

Nicky felt a chill go through her as she heard the woman's words. It was so sudden. Just like the recording.

"I knew she was dead right away," the woman said. "That's when I screamed, and you two arrived shortly after..." The woman shivered. "Do you think someone murdered her?"

Nicky looked over at the docks, where the officers had finished extracting the body from the water. Nicky couldn't see a clear cause of death yet.

"We can't be sure," she told the woman, even though she was pretty damn sure. "What's your name, ma'am?"

"Angela," the woman replied. "Angela Green."

"Do you live here in the Bahamas?" Nicky asked, her mind spinning with questions.

Angela nodded. "Yes, I live here in Wahoe Bay. I come down to the docks every day to watch the boats come in."

"And do you know anyone who would want to hurt this woman?" Ken asked. "Any history of violence in this area?"

Angela shook her head. "No, no one I can think of. It's such a tragedy, I can't imagine why anyone would do this. We don't have a lot of violence here at all."

"Do you know who she is?" Nicky asked, trying to keep her voice steady.

The woman shook her head again. "No, I don't. I've never seen her before."

Nicky nodded, her mind racing. So, the body had been dumped here, but who had put it here? And what did it have to do with Delilah?

Suddenly, Nicky heard a voice from behind her.

"You two should come with me," a gruff voice said.

Nicky and Ken turned to see a man dressed in a police uniform, a determined expression on his face.

"I need to talk to you about something," the man said.

Nicky and Ken exchanged a look, both feeling a wave of dread come over them.

"What is it?" Nicky asked, her voice barely above a whisper.

The man cleared his throat and gestured for them to follow. Nicky nodded at Angela before following after the officer. They moved toward the docks, then stopped right before them. The officer sighed as he met Nicky's eyes. She wondered what he was so hesitant to say and held her breath, awaiting his response.

"The victim--she's known to us," he said.

Nicky's stomach dropped. She exchanged a look with Ken.

"What? How?" Ken asked.

"Her name is June, and she's been known to prostitute downtown," the officer explained. "She's been in and out of trouble with the law for years, but no one knows much about her. We think she was living on the streets and had recently become involved with a gang." He shook his head sadly. "It's a shame--she was so young."

Nicky's heart sank for June. This wasn't fair for anyone.

"Do you know who could have done this?" Nicky asked, her voice strained.

The officer shook his head. "No, we don't. We'll be searching the area and talking to the locals, but right now, we don't have any leads. We'll look into June's clients too, if we can track any of them."

Nicky nodded, then glanced over at June's body, now on the dock, drying under the afternoon sun. "I'd like to take a look at the body," she said.

The officer nodded. "Go ahead," he said, gesturing to the body.

Nicky and Ken both stepped closer to the body, their eyes widening in shock as they took in the horrific sight. June's skin was pale and lifeless, her eyes still open with a look of terror frozen on her face. Her clothes were tattered and torn, evidence of a struggle that had taken place before her death. They could see bruises on her arms and legs as well, further proof that she had been brutally attacked. The cause of death, from what Nicky could tell, was multiple stab wounds to her torso. -

Nicky felt a wave of sadness wash over her as she stared at June's lifeless body. She could only imagine what kind of person would do something so cruel and heartless - to take someone's life away in such an abrupt and violent way. Nicky glanced up at the sky for a moment before turning back to Ken, who looked equally as distraught by what they were seeing.

Suddenly, Nicky noticed something glinting from June's pocket. She put a latex glove on, then bent down and carefully pulled out a small wallet.

Inside the wallet, Nicky found a few pictures of June, smiling and happy. There was also a bus ticket, an ID card and some cash. But what caught her attention most was a small piece of paper with a phone number scribbled on it. Nicky furrowed her brows as she stared at the number, wondering who it belonged to and if it could have anything to do with June's death.

Nicky glanced up at Ken, her expression grim. "We need to find out who this number belongs to," she said. Ken took out his phone and programmed it into it. Once they had the number, Nicky dropped the wallet into an evidence bag and handed it to one of the officers standing by.

"Make sure forensics does a full sweep of everything she has," Nicky said.

The officer nodded and took the bag.

Nicky and Ken looked at each other, both knowing what they had to do next. They needed to find a private spot where they could call the number without anyone overhearing them. With a silent agreement, they set off down the dock, looking for a secluded area away from prying eyes and ears. They stopped under the shade of a tree.

"Well, let's call it," Nicky said to Ken.

Ken nodded and took out his phone and dialed the number, then put it on speaker. He held his breath as the phone began to ring, expecting a voicemail or some automated response. But instead, a man answered on the other end.

"Hello?"

Nicky and Ken paused, exchanging a glance. That voice was familiar.

"Hello?" Nicky said.

A pause. "Who is this? How did you get this number?"

The voice sounded familiar, and as Nicky listened, she suddenly realized who it was.

"Henry Minns," she said quietly. "It's you."

"Yes, this is my personal cell... so again, how did you get this number?"

Nicky's stomach bottomed out. Henry Minns, the same guy who had held the rally here. The mayor of Wahoe Bay, who was running for re-election.

His number was in a dead woman's wallet.

Ken gave Nicky a look, as if asking her what to do. On a whim, she reached out and hung up the phone.

"Hey, why'd you do that?" Ken asked.

"Ken, it's Henry Minns," Nicky said. "His number was in June's wallet. We have to figure out how to handle this."

Ken placed his finger on his chin in thought. "Do you think he was one of her clients? He was soliciting sex from her?"

Nicky shook her head. "I don't know, but that's what we have to find out. We need to talk to him first and see what he knows."

Nicky and Ken looked at each other, both knowing what they had to do. They had to confront Henry Minns and get some answers. They had to find out why June had his number and if he had anything to do with her death.

But they needed a game plan. Henry should be back at his office after the rally, and Nicky knew he would have all of his confidants around too, and his staff. They should talk to them first, and see if Henry had any history of violence or creepy behavior toward women.

It didn't quite add up for him to be the one to send the recording, since he was making a speech at the time. But he could have had someone else do it for him. He also could have killed June before he got on stage, leaving her in the water to be found.

Nicky nodded. "We'll have to be careful when we confront him," she said. "We don't know what he's capable of yet. We might learn more if we interrogate his staff before him."

Ken nodded in agreement. "Let's get going then," he said. "We don't have much time."

They set off, jogging toward the rental car. As they did, Nicky's mind swam with possibilities. If Henry was the killer--and kidnapper--then it would be a huge scandal for Wahoe Bay. A beloved mayor turned killer... Nicky could see the headlines now.

But there was no time to think of that right now. They had to find June's killer before it was too late. As far as they knew, Delilah was with the same man who had killed June.

If Nicky didn't act soon, Delilah would be next.

CHAPTER FOURTEEN

Nicky and Ken drove to Henry's office, both of them tense and quiet as Nicky drove. Nicky was trying to put together a plan in her head, but her thoughts were jumbled and chaotic. What if Henry was the killer? Or what if he had hired someone else to do it? If so--why?

Most vexing of all--how and why was the killer contacting Nicky?

First, he knew her personal address. Then, her personal cell.

This was a sick, twisted game he was playing, and if Henry was the culprit, then Nicky would lock him behind bars for a long, long time.

Before the drive, Nicky had done some quick recon on Henry Minns. He was born in Wahoe Bay and had a wife with two children. He had been in politics his whole life, but he was only forty years old and became mayor in his late thirties.

He was known for his charm and charisma, which made it all the more disturbing if he was the killer. How could someone so charming and likable be capable of such a heinous crime?

Nicky shook her head to clear her thoughts as she pulled into the parking lot of Henry's office building. She found a parking spot and faced Ken, who looked nervously at the building.

"Ready?" Nicky asked.

Ken nodded. "Let's do this," he said, and opened his door to get out of the car.

Nicky followed suit, and they made their way toward Henry's office building. They stopped at the entrance, taking in the grandeur of the building. It was a tall structure with yellow walls and pristinely landscaped gardens surrounding it.

Nickie took a deep breath before pushing open the doors to enter. Inside, they were greeted by an elegant lobby with dark wood paneling and polished floors. They were met with a flurry of activity. Henry's staff was scurrying around, trying to prepare for the upcoming election. As Nicky and Ken stepped inside, a few of the staff members glanced at them suspiciously, but moved on with their tasks.

Nicky took a deep breath and approached the receptionist. She was an older woman with a stern face, her hands clasped tightly in her lap.

"Excuse me," Nicky said. "We're looking for Henry Minns. Is he in?"

The receptionist nodded without meeting Nicky's gaze. "He is, but he's busy right now."

Nicky paused, debating whether or not to press further. She glanced at Ken who gave her a slight nod of encouragement.

"I understand that," Nicky said slowly. "But I need to talk to him about something important. It's about his campaign."

She saw the receptionist tense up and her lips quiver slightly. It made Nicky pause for a moment before continuing on, determined to get some answers from Henry even if it meant making the receptionist uncomfortable in the process.

"Has Henry ever made you feel uncomfortable?" Nicky asked firmly, locking eyes with the woman across from her. The receptionist hesitated for a moment before finally shaking her head no and averting her gaze again.

"Of course not," the receptionist said. "Henry is a great man, and a great mayor."

But there was something about her expression that made Nicky wary--it almost seemed like she was hiding something from them, or trying not to give away too much information about Henry's behavior towards women in general.

"Are you sure?" Nicky asked. She glanced at Ken, then subtly flashed her FBI badge.

The girl's eyes widened. "FBI? What are you doing here?"

"Don't worry about that for now," Ken said, leaning against the counter. "Just know that you can trust us. If there's anything about Henry you think we should know, now would be the time."

The receptionist stared at them for a few moments, then finally nodded her head.

"Henry is a good man," she said firmly. "He's never made me feel uncomfortable or done anything inappropriate."

Nicky still felt uneasy. It seemed like the receptionist was holding something back--but what? She decided to press on and see if she could get any more information out of the woman.

"And did you ever see him with any women? Anyone other than his wife?"

The receptionist hesitated for a moment, then shook her head. "No, I don't think so," she said. "He's always been very professional around here."

Nicky nodded, feeling some relief. It seemed unlikely that Henry was the killer if he was as professional as the receptionist said. But she still felt uneasy. Something was off, and she wanted to be sure before they confronted Henry.

"Thank you," Nicky said. "Do you know when he'll be finished with his work?"

The receptionist checked her watch. "He should be finished in a few minutes," she said. "Would you like me to call him for you?"

Nicky shook her head. "No, that won't be necessary," she said. "We'll wait."

The receptionist nodded, then went back to her work. Nicky and Ken took a seat in the lobby to wait for Henry's arrival. As they sat there, Nicky's mind raced with questions. Was Henry the killer? Or was someone else involved? She wanted to know the truth, no matter what it was.

A few minutes later, Henry emerged from his office. He was a tall man with graying hair and a stern expression. As he walked past Nicky and Ken, he barely acknowledged their presence.

Nickie stood up and followed him, her heart pounding in her chest. She didn't know what to expect when she confronted him, but she was determined to get the answers she needed.

"Henry Minns!" she called out.

Henry glanced at her in surprise, then narrowed his eyes. "Can I help you?" he asked.

"We need to speak with you about June," Nicky said. "I'm Nicky, and this is my partner, Ken. Do you remember us?"

Henry's lips pursed. "Of course," he said. "I just don't see why you need to speak with me now. I'm very busy."

"Are you sure you don't want to deal with this now?" Ken asked. "Or do you want to wait?"

Henry shook his head. "I want to wait," he said. "I'm very busy right now with my campaign. Go talk to my wife if you have questions. She'll be more than happy to help you."

Nicky felt an icy chill in her gut. Why would Henry be so eager to send them to his wife? Could he really have done something to June?

"Are you sure we can't talk to you now?" she asked. "It's important."

Henry sighed, as though he was exasperated with Nicky's persistence. But then, she flashed her FBI badge, along with Ken. Henry's expression darkened.

"Fine," he said, "we can talk in my office."

He led them into a luxurious office with a large mahogany desk. He sat behind the desk, then pointed to two chairs in front of it. Nicky and Ken sat down and stared at Henry expectantly.

"What is this about?" Henry said. "I'm very busy."

Nicky glanced at Ken, then cleared her throat. "Mr. Minns, were you informed of the reason your rally was cleared earlier today?"

Henry shook his head. "I don't know, some sort of criminal activity," he said.

"Is that what you told the police?" Nicky asked.

Henry shrugged. "I don't see why it matters," he said. "What is this about?"

"A woman was found dead by the docks," Nicky said. She exchanged a glance with Ken again. "And we think you might have something to do with it."

Henry scoffed. "I have no idea what you're talking about," he said. "I'm a very busy man. I would have nothing to do with any poor woman being found dead anywhere."

And yet he didn't seem so remorseful. It seemed all that garbage Henry was spewing about being a "voice for the people" went away when he wasn't performing on stage.

"This number was found in her wallet," Nicky said. She took out a piece of paper, which she'd scribed the number on, and showed it to Henry.

All at once, his face fell. "That's... you." He frowned at Nicky in realization. "You're the one who called me earlier."

"I was," Nicky said. She nodded at Ken, who took her cue. He took out his phone and brought up a picture of June--when she was alive--flashing it at Henry.

"Do you know this woman?" Ken asked. "Her name is June Peterson."

Henry averted his eyes, a telltale sign of guilt. "No," he said firmly. "I don't know who she is."

Nicky narrowed her eyes, studying Henry's face. He seemed to be telling the truth, but there was something in his voice that made her doubt him.

"Are you sure?" Nicky asked. "You didn't know her by any other name? Maybe a nickname?"

Henry's face hardened and he shook his head again. "No," he said firmly. "I've never heard of this woman before in my life."

"And yet your personal number was written down on a piece of paper in her wallet," Nicky pointed out.

Henry's face blanched. "That's impossible," he said. "You must have the wrong man."

"I have the right man," Nicky said. "There's no doubt about that."

"But I don't know her," Henry insisted. "She's just some random woman. I can't explain what her number is doing in her wallet, but I'm telling you I never met the woman."

Nicky stared at him for a long moment, trying to decide if he was telling the truth. She could tell from his expression that he was terrified and she couldn't help but feel a twinge of pity for him. He had something to do with June's death, she was sure of it, but she still wasn't sure what.

"We'll need to search your office," Ken said suddenly. "Just in case."

Henry shook his head vehemently. "No," he said. "That's too much. You can't just come in here and start snooping around."

"It's important," Nicky said gently. "We have to find out what happened to June and we need your help."

Henry sighed heavily, looking defeated. He knew there would be no way out of this mess now and he reluctantly agreed to let them search his office. As they searched through drawers and cabinets, Nicky couldn't help but feel a deep sense of dread about what they might find or not find. There were so many unanswered questions surrounding June's death and Nicky had a feeling that Henry Minns knew more than he was letting on.

"This is preposterous," Henry said. "You aren't going to find anything in here."

Nicky and Ken exchanged a look and continued searching, but after several minutes of rummaging through drawers and filing cabinets, it became increasingly clear that Henry was right. They found nothing of significance in his office. Nicky sighed in frustration, her hopes of finding something to help June's case diminishing.

Just then, someone knocked on the office door. Nicky turned around to find a boy, probably no older than nineteen, standing there with a worried expression on his face. "Dad," he said slowly. "What's going on?"

Henry huffed. "These FBI agents think my personal number was in some dead woman's wallet. Ridiculous!"

The boy's face fell. "What woman?"

That caught Nicky's attention--something about the way the boy looked suddenly guilty, as if he knew something.

"Her name is June," Nicky said. She stepped forward and showed the boy the photo, and his face went as white as a sheet.

"S-she's dead?"

"Do you know her?" Ken asked, stepping forward and crossing his arms.

The boy looked from Ken to Nicky and then finally at his father, who gave him a slight nod. "Yes," he said, his voice barely above a whisper. "I gave her my dad's number."

CHAPTER FIFTEEN

Nicky couldn't believe what she had just heard. Henry's son stared timidly at the ground, but said nothing more, and Nicky shared a look with both Henry and Ken. This didn't make any sense. Why would Henry's son give June--a homeless prostitute--his father's personal number?

Could this just be a ruse to protect his dad?

"What do you mean?" Nicky asked.

"David," Henry cut in, but David raised a hand.

"She was a ginger-haired woman, right?" David asked.

Nicky nodded, although this only further added to her confusion. She pulled up the photo of June on her hone and showed it to David, and his face went pale. He swallowed hard, guilt written all over his expression.

"I-I saw her the other day when I was walking home from my friend's at night," David said. "She was running from someone... or something... I don't know. She stopped me in the street, and I thought she was high on something. We were totally alone."

Nicky imagined this situation in her head. It seemed plausible, but what was June running from?

The kidnapper?

"She begged me for help," David said. "She said she needed a place to stay and some money. I didn't have anything for her, but I--I wanted to help..."

Henry stepped up, his expression furious. "And what does this have to do with me?"

"I gave her your number, Dad," David said. "I said you were someone who could help set her up with a shelter. I didn't say you were the mayor, I just... I knew that if anyone could help her, it would be you, Dad."

Henry's face was beet red and Nicky could tell that this was a hard pill for him to swallow. He was a proud man, and didn't want to be personally associated with included drug addicts and prostitutes. June was allegedly both of those things.

"Oh, David," Henry said sadly. "Why would you be so stupid? You gave this girl money?"

David shook his head. "No," he said. "I didn't give her any money. I don't have any money. I gave her your number and then I went home. She was alone, Dad. She was literally begging me for help. I thought she could tell you and since you're the mayor, you could help her."

"You should have called the police," Henry said, then sighed. "This is completely my fault. I run my campaign on being there for everyone, but I'm not always like that. I'm sorry, son."

David shook his head. "You told me before you can help people like her," he said. "I thought that meant you would help her. You wouldn't let anyone else call the cops on her."

Nicky frowned. What was all this about?

"David, I'm sorry," Henry said. "I didn't mean for her to get hurt."

"But she's dead," David said. "If I had just stayed with her..."

"She never even called me," Henry said. "You can't blame yourself for this."

Nicky shared a look with Ken. That was enough family talk for now--Nicky was more concerned about why June had seemed so scared.

"Was she running from someone that night?" Nicky asked.

David shook his head. "I don't know," he said. "She just said that she needed to get out of there. She said she was in danger. I didn't know what to do, so I gave her your number."

"And you never saw her again?" Nicky asked.

David shook his head. "Not that I know of."

"Did she tell you anything else?" Nicky asked. "About where she came from? Or her name?"

David shook his head. "She was high," he said. "She was out of it. I don't think she even knew who she was."

Nicky frowned. That didn't sound good. He needed to figure out more about June and what she was running from.

"Did she mention anyone else?" Nicky asked. "Anyone she was afraid of? Or any other places she might have been staying?"

David shook his head again. "No," he said, looking down at the ground. "I'm sorry, I don't know anything else."

Nicky nodded, trying to process all of this information. If David was telling the truth, it seemed like June had been on the run for some reason, but what that reason was still remained a mystery. She looked up at David and Henry, both of them looking so sad and helpless in the face of this tragedy that had unfolded before them. Nicky mulled this over, considering all the possibilities. If June had been running from someone, then that person could have been the one to kill her.

That would certainly explain the way she looked--defeated.

"I have another question," Nicky said.

The two men looked at her, and David nodded. Nicky's eyes flicked to the picture of June again, and then back to David's face. "What did June look like when you met her?" Nicky asked.

David refocused his eyes and looked to Nicky. "She was dirty. She looked like she had been sleeping in a trash can, or something," he said. "But she was a beautiful woman. I never would have guessed her to be... a prostitute. She had this innocence about her. Even after she told me what she did for a living, I couldn't believe it. I just... she didn't seem like the type of woman who would do that."

Nicky nodded, still staring at the picture of June. He wondered if David would have given her money if he had known she was a prostitute. Would he have even taken the time to try and help her?

"Did she have a backpack?" Ken asked.

David shook his head. "No," he said. "It was like she had nothing on her."

Nicky glanced back up at David and his father, who were both looking at her with concerned expressions, as though worried they were still suspects. Unfortunately for David, it seemed as though he was the last person to see June Peterson alive.

"David, where were you earlier today, during your father's rally by the beach?"

David's eyes widened slightly, and he glanced over at his father before looking back to Nicky. "I was with my friends," he said. "We were down by the pier all morning." He looked away, a hint of sadness in his voice. It was clear that June Peterson had made an impact on him, and not just because she had been murdered.

"Can someone confirm that?" Ken asked.

David nodded. "Yes," he said. "I was with my friends, they'll tell you."

"Do you have their contact information?" Nicky asked. "I'd like to talk to them."

"Of course," David said. He went over to the desk and grabbed a sheet of paper, writing down some names and numbers, then handed it to Nicky.

Nicky stared at him for a moment, then turned away. In truth, she was furious, more furious than she had been in a long time, but she didn't know what the hell she was angry at. She wasn't really angry at David, but just this whole situation. She was angry at the fact that June had been so lonely and scared that she couldn't even ask a family member for help. She was angry at how tragic the situation was, and she was even angry at the fact that she wasn't angry at David. She didn't care that he was a guy who just wanted to help women on the streets. David could have saved June's life, but he left her.

There was nothing they could do now, though. June was gone, but Delilah was still out there. They could still save her.

"Thank you for your time," Nicky said. "I really appreciate it."

She and Ken headed for the door.

"That's it?" Henry asked.

Nicky looked over her shoulder at David and Henry, who were watching her with absolute confusion on their faces. "Yeah," she said. "We'll be in touch if we need more."

***

Nicky and Ken walked out of the office, into the warm day. The Bahamas sun was shining brightly in the sky, casting long shadows across the sand and making it sparkle like tiny diamonds. The salty smell of the ocean wafted through the open door, tickling Nicky's nose as they stepped out. As beautiful as Wahoe Bay was--her head was pounding.

They would confirm his alibi, but it looked like neither David--nor Henry--were the kidnapper they were looking for.

"This case just keeps getting more and more confusing," she said.

"Agreed," Ken said. "What do you think is going on here? What does this have to do with the murders?"

Nicky chewed on her lip thoughtfully. "I think June Peterson was running from someone," she said. "But she was using the same drugs too, so maybe she was on them when she was killed."

"So, June was probably high," Ken said.

Nicky nodded. It made sense. She had been running from someone, someone who had killed her. Nicky wondered if that person was the same person who had taken Delilah. But if he was killing women so fast, then why was Delilah still alive? Was there something that made her different from the rest of the girls? Delilah had gone missing from

Miami six months ago. June had only gone missing a couple of days ago, and she was already dead.

What was the killer planning?

Nicky felt a chill go down her spine. She knew what they had to do now. They had to find out who this killer was and stop him before he could hurt anyone else. But how?

"We need more information," she said, turning to Ken. "Let's start by looking into June's family, see if they know anything. It's unclear to me if she even has any on the island. Maybe June knew the killer."

A lot of things about this case were unclear, and it made Nicky's head hurt. The only thing that was certain was that if they didn't find Delilah soon, she could suffer the same fate as June.

Nicky just hoped that it wasn't already too late.

CHAPTER SIXTEEN

He had made a terrible mistake.

As he drove through the island, he looked in his rearview mirror and caught sight of Delilah in the back of his car, her mouth taped over and her hands tied. With his wonderfully tinted windows, there was no hope of her being seen. Her singing wasn't good enough after all. After disposing of June, he'd realized how sick he'd grown of Delilah's voice over the past several months.

Her voice wasn't good enough to be his.

So, he needed another. Another voice to add, to choose from. Someone to beat Delilah.

Another voice, one to better represent the beauty inside of him, the beauty he couldn't express himself.

He knew what he had to do.

The plan was simple, but dangerous. He would have to find someone who could sing better than Delilah, and then he would kidnap them. Once they were in his possession, he would force them to sing for him until they were exhausted and broken. It seemed the only way to get the voice he wanted and needed so desperately.

He drove through the island, keeping an eye out for anyone who might fit the bill; someone with a beautiful voice that could match his own inner beauty. As he drove, he formulated a plan as to how this person would be taken and forced into singing against their will: He planned on following them around until they stopped somewhere alone, then subduing them quickly before they had time to scream or alert anyone else of their presence – it would have to be done fast if it was going to work at all.

He began to formulate a plan. He knew exactly who he wanted. Someone whose voice was so powerful it could melt hearts and fill the silent void in his life. He thought of her every day, often recalling it during his long nightly drives around the island.

He would find her, no matter what it took. She was too far away for him to just pick up and take, so he decided to take matters into his own hands: kidnapping was the only option left. It would be a risk, but one he was willing to take if it meant getting the voice he desired so badly.

In the back seat, Delilah made noises through her gag. No voice for her today. He shook his head to silently communicate with her.

No, Delilah. You're not good enough.

He stopped his car at the edge of the park. There were often singers here. He saw a woman standing on the side of the street, singing with a ukelele. Maybe she could be the one. Someone who could sing like her, who could match his beauty, his passion, his desire.

He watched her from his car, studying her movements and the way she held herself. He watched as she sang a song, her voice radiating through the daytime air like liquid gold.

He watched her from his car, studying her every move. He wanted to be sure she was the one and he wanted to make sure he had enough time to take her when the moment arose. He felt a surge of adrenaline.

The woman seemed oblivious to him, unaware of the danger she was in. How could someone so beautiful be unaware of how precious their voice was? He watched as she laughed with friends, sang and hummed along to music--all without knowing that soon, that voice would be stolen away by him.

He glanced back at Delilah. He'd had such high hopes for her, and she had kept him happy for the months she'd been with him, until her voice had grown stale. He wanted to be heard by someone marvelous, someone who would really grab the attention of everyone, someone who demanded to be listened to.

He listened to the woman's voice for a moment longer...

No...

It wasn't good enough.

Not enough to get the attention of that FBI agent, Nicky Lyons. He'd heard her voice on the news. It was so sultry and smooth...

That was the perfect voice.

Was she here, he wondered? Had she followed his clues?

He turned his head to the right. Across the street, he saw a young woman with blonde hair. He watched her for a moment, and then noticed that she was humming to herself. She looked perfectly normal, and perfectly at home with her voice.

No. Still not good enough.

He continued to drive around the island, looking here and there, watching for the voice of his dreams. The perfect voice.

The perfect girl.

The perfect woman.

She was out there somewhere. He would find her, no matter what. He would abduct her and force her to sing for him until she gave up. He would force her to use her voice until she was exhausted, until she gave up and submitted to him. That was the only way he could be satisfied.

He turned his head back to the woman singing with the ukelele. She was better, but still not quite what he was looking for.

He continued driving around the park, studying the people who were there to enjoy the day. He watched them all, and then he saw it: a young woman who was too thin to be healthy, with long red hair he could run his fingers through as he listened to her voice.

She was singing to herself with a soft voice, and as he watched her and listened to her, he saw her thin fingers move over her guitar and he felt his heart melt.

She was perfect. Just perfect.

He followed her for another minute, making sure that she was truly the one he wanted. He watched her for a long time, and he listened to her voice.

She was perfect. He had to have her.

He turned his head to Delilah in the back seat and shook it.

No.

He decided to take his chance.

He would strike when she was alone.

When she was unaware, and unable to defend herself.

He felt his heart race as he pulled into a parking space.

He watched her as she turned her head to her left and stopped singing.

She was truly perfect.

And she would be his new voice.

CHAPTER SEVENTEEN

Nicky pulled the rental car up to a small house on the outskirts of Wahoe Bay, Ken in the passenger seat. The street was lined with dilapidated houses, most of them in need of repairs. The houses were surrounded by clusters of coconut trees and a variety of flowering plants, all in various stages of decay. A small market sat off to the side, selling fruit and other staples. Further down the street, she could see a few small boats docked at a pier, bobbing in the shallow waters.

This was a rough end of town, and as it turned out, June did have family here.

Her mother lived in this house. Nicky could only imagine what kind of relationship they had that June would ask a total stranger for help and a place to stay over her own mother.

"Poor June," Nicky muttered.

Ken looked out at the house too. "Yeah. Seems she had it rough in life."

Nicky couldn't help but feel a bit of pity for June. Homeless, turned to drugs and prostitution, even though she lived on this beautiful island. And in the end, she had been senselessly murdered.

Nicky opened the car door and got out, stretching her arms and legs. The rental car was cramped, but at least it felt nice and cool inside. It was humid outside, and the heat was oppressive.

She looked at the house in front of her. It wasn't much to look at. The paint was peeling off the walls, and the grass was overgrown. The windows were covered with curtains made of faded lace, and it looked as if no one had taken care of the place in a very long time.

Nicky sighed and followed Ken up to the front door. She rang the doorbell twice. After a few minutes, an older woman opened it. She was frail, with gray hair and tired eyes. She looked like she had been through a lot in life, but when she saw Nicky and Ken standing there, her face softened into a gentle smile. She surely was already informed of June's passing by the local police, and there were tears drying on her cheeks. Despite that, she gave off a warm aura.

"Can I help you?" she said softly.

Nicky held up her badge, along with Ken. "Are you Mrs. Peterson?"

"I am," she said. "Mary... I'm sure you're here about my June. You can come in, if you'd like."

Nicky shared a look with Ken, then nodded, stepping inside the home. It smelled of cigarettes, but also something warmer, like candles burning.

The living room was cozy, despite its shabby appearance. An old sofa sat against one wall with some blankets tossed over it; the walls were covered in pictures of June at various stages of her life -- from infancy to young adulthood -- as well as photos of other family members.

"June was always so talented musically," Mary said, sitting down on the floral couch. Nicky and Ken sat on the loveseat next to her. "She could pick up any instrument quickly, and her singing voice was beyond compare..."

Based on the state of the home, and how Mary spoke of June, Nicky might think they had a good relationship. But that didn't seem to be the case. "Do you mind if I ask what your relationship with June was like?" Nicky asked. "From what we understand, she didn't have a home."

Mary looked away and sighed. "June was always a difficult child. She was always so full of life, but it seemed she could never find the right path. Eventually, she got into drugs, and that's when our relationship became strained." Mary shook her head sadly. "I wanted to help her, but I just didn't know how. Every time I tried to talk to her about it, she just ran away or lashed out at me. It wasn't until recently that she started coming around more often and talking with me again. She even came and visited a few weeks ago, stayed in her old bedroom. But then... it was too late."

Nicky could barely contain her emotions as Mary spoke; there were tears in the older woman's eyes as the memories flooded back to her. Nicky knew that Mary had gone through a lot of pain trying to take care of June, especially with the added stress of addiction -- something no parent should ever have to deal with. She wanted so much for June to get better and live a happy life, but unfortunately it just wasn't in the cards for them both.

"She was in and out of rehab centers and various programs, but nothing seemed to stick," Mary said sadly. "It was hard for me because I wanted so much for June to get better, but every time I thought she had turned the corner, things just got worse." Nicky could see the pain in her eyes as she spoke about her daughter's struggles with drugs -- there were no simple answers or quick fixes in this situation. All that Mary could do was try to be supportive of June while keeping her distance enough not to enable her addiction.

"We're very sorry to hear about that," Nicky said. "Did June have any enemies that you knew of? Any men who bothered her?"

Mary sighed. "I'm sure there were many. June's... choice of work came with risks. I'm assuming one of her 'clients' did this to her."

"We actually have evidence to suggest it may have been someone else," Ken said. "Someone who wasn't a client."

"Really?" Mary's brows pinched. "Who, then?"

"We aren't completely certain yet," Nicky said. "That's why we wanted to talk to you. To see if you could point us in any direction."

Mary shook her head. "I'm sorry, I don't know who could have done this to her. June was... she was so young and had so much potential. But it seemed like no matter what she did, bad luck followed her." Mary wiped a tear away from her cheek. "I just wish I knew who killed my daughter."

Nicky and Ken both stood up, thanking Mary for her time. "We're very sorry for your loss," Nicky said softly. "Do you mind if we look in June's old bedroom? Maybe there's something useful in there that she left the last time she was here."

Mary nodded, leading the way upstairs. She opened the door to June's old bedroom and stepped aside, allowing Nicky and Ken to enter first.

"I never changed it from when June was a teenager," Mary clarified.

The room was surprisingly well kept, with the bed neatly made and the walls adorned with pictures of June and her friends. Nicky could feel the sadness in the air; June had obviously been living a difficult life before her death. On the dresser, there was a small notebook with a pen tucked into the binding. Nicky picked it up and opened it, flipping through the pages. She could see that it was full of June's thoughts and musings, her hopes and dreams for the future from when she was young and naïve.

On the nightstand, there was a small jewelry box with a few pieces of jewelry inside. Nicky opened it and saw a locket with a picture of June and Mary inside. She ran her finger over the picture. She closed the jewelry box and placed it back on the nightstand before turning to the wall behind the bed. There was a large painting of a beautiful flower garden, and Nicky could feel the warmth and beauty of it radiating from the canvas.

Mary pointed at the dresser across from the bed. "That was June's favorite piece of furniture," she said. "She always kept it neat and tidy. Everything else in her life was chaos, but she loved this thing."

Nicky and Ken walked over and opened the drawers, finding a few clothes and some trinkets inside. But nothing seemed to stand out as being important.

Mary walked over to the closet and opened the door. Inside was a box filled with old letters, photographs, and other mementos. "She kept all her memories here," Mary said, her voice barely above a whisper. Nicky and Ken went through the box, but nothing seemed to be out of the ordinary.

Mary smiled sadly as she closed the closet door. "June may have been gone, but I still feel her presence in this room," she said. "It's like she's still here with us. I've always felt that way, even when things got hard."

It was a sad story, one that resonated with Nicky deeply. She wished she could have done more for June while she was alive.

"We'll do everything we can to get justice for June," Nicky said. "It's obvious you loved her."

Mary nodded, a faint smile on her lips. "Thank you. Please let me know if there's anything else I can do to help."

Nicky and Ken thanked Mary again and gave her their contact information before leaving the home, filled with memories of June. As they walked away, Nicky couldn't help but feel a heavy sadness in her heart; it was clear that June had been loved by many people throughout her life, but she would never get the chance to make something of herself.

It was too late for her, but it wasn't too late for Delilah.

They had to go back to the drawing board.

***

Back at the hotel room, Nicky sat at the table, her mind mulling over the details of the case. Ken was out grabbing them dinner, and through the windows of the hotel, the shadows were growing longer across the beach. It was getting into the evening, and they still had no solid leads.

Nicky was starting to get frustrated. With all the clues, they should have been able to figure out who had killed June by now -- but they were no closer to a solution than they had been the day before.

That was the problem with this case. There were too many clues, and they didn't know how to connect the dots.

There were not enough suspects and not enough evidence, and Nicky just couldn't get a handle on it. She was out of her element, and it was frustrating her to no end.

Nicky took a deep breath and closed her eyes, making a concerted effort to calm down. She couldn't be sure she was going about this the right way. Maybe there was a better way to crack this case open, but she didn't know what it was.

What did she have to work with? The most obvious lead was the fact that the killer had been contacting Nicky himself, and had been toying with her.

Was he some sort of hacker? She still had no idea how he had been able to obtain her personal information. Perhaps they could narrow their search to people who worked in tech, but that felt so broad.

The door opened, and Ken stepped in, a small plastic bag in his hand. "Got us some dinner," he said, setting the bag down on the table.

"Thanks," Nicky said. "I was starting to get a bit hungry."

"I know how that goes," Ken said as he pulled out a hamburger and some fries.

Nicky grabbed a burger of her own and they both began to eat, the smell of the food filling the room with a comforting aroma. As they ate, she looked out at the beach and watched as the sun slowly set in the sky, painting it with streaks of orange and pink. June had watched the sunset here. She wondered if Delilah ever got to see it too, or if she was holed up in some basement somewhere, never to see the light of day.

Her mind wandered back to the case. There had to be something she was missing. Some angle she hadn't quite worked yet.

They had the recordings. Could there be a clue in them she had missed?

Each had a woman's voice, and each had a man talking--or singing--in the background.

She thought about what Joe Rockwater's song had contained. The lyrics. "Lost her voice..."

A sudden thought struck her.

Hold on...

Henry Minns's speech--it also used the word 'voice.'

"I know that look," Ken said, and Nicky met his eyes as her mind raced to form a theory. "What are you thinking?"

It all came together in one dizzying moment.

"Henry Minns's speech," she said. "He used the word voice. So did Joe in the background of the recording."

Her heart was pounding with excitement as a possibility began to form. Could there be a connection here?

Nicky's mind started to race. As an FBI agent, she had years of experiencing dealing with the strange and wicked minds of the world. Sometimes, even a small detail could be the most significant. This one stood out.

Voice... why would he be fixated on that word?

Did he not like his own voice? That was possible. Maybe that was why he was sending Nicky recordings of other people's voices.

Or maybe it went even deeper than that. Nicky's mind began to swirl down different paths, her years of experience building up, reminding her of all the deranged killers she'd taken down in her lifetime.

Maybe the killer had no voice. Maybe he was completely mute. That could explain why he was so obsessed with other people's voices, why he was so intent on sending Nicky recordings of them. He wanted to hear something he could never have.

It was a chilling thought, but one that made a lot of sense.

If the killer was mute, it would explain why he never made contact with Nicky directly. It would explain why he never revealed himself. He had no way of doing so.

It seemed to fit. The killer had no voice. He was a ghost, a shadow, haunting them from the shadows. But even ghosts could be caught.

Ken frowned at Nicky. "So? What are you thinking"

"What if the recordings were meant to send a message? What if the killer was trying to tell us something?" Nicky asked, her mind spinning with possibilities. "He keeps using the word voice..." She paused and met Ken's eyes. "What if he doesn't have one?"

CHAPTER EIGHTEEN

Maybe it was a longshot--but at least they had something to go off now.

Nicky had her laptop open in the hotel room, with Ken across from her, and they both typed away as they searched through databases, trying to find anyone with a criminal record, who also happened to be mute or have speech issues.

They weren't limiting themselves to Wahoe Bay. The killer could live on a different island in the Bahamas, or he might have moved here from America. Nicky couldn't forget that Delilah was originally kidnapped in Miami, but it seemed she'd been brought here. Either way, their search was broad, which gave them a lot more to look at.

As she searched, Nicky couldn't help but feel like they were getting closer. There were thousands of results on the database she was using, but every new name she found felt like progress. She couldn't help but feel like they were going to find something--anything--to lead them to Delilah.

"What about this guy?" Ken asked, and Nicky looked up to see him pointing at the screen.

"Mason Thomas," Nicky muttered, reading the file on her computer. "Convicted of assault five years ago. Born mute. Lives in Wahoe Bay..."

"I don't know much about that case yet," Ken said. "You want me to dig deeper?"

"Yeah, go ahead," Nicky said, leaning back. "He seems promising. I'll keep looking."

She kept scrolling through the database, her fingers flying across the keyboard as she took in every detail of every file as quickly as she humanly could.

She wanted to find Delilah--she wanted to find her more than she cared about anything else at the moment.

This was the only way she could get justice for June. And she had to get it right this time.

Her eyes were straining as she scrolled down. She still couldn't see anything that stood out to her. She wouldn't be able to sleep until they found something.

She had to find something.

"Wait," Ken said suddenly, and Nicky looked up at him. "I think I've got something on Marcus..." Ken sighed. "He's not our guy."

Nicky frowned. "Are you sure? But--"

"He's been out of the country for weeks," Ken said. "It's not him."

Nicky sighed, truthfully not surprised. Things were never that simple for them. "Back to the drawing board."

She focused on her laptop. She wasn't even sure what she was looking for, but she hoped that something would jump out at her.

She typed in a new search term, this time narrowing down her focus to the files of people who had been convicted of assault, but had received light sentences.

The database gave her thousands of results, and her heart sank a little. She knew that she couldn't look at them all--that would be absolutely impossible.

She stopped to think. How could she narrow down the database?

She typed in 'assault with a deadly weapon' and the database returned hundreds and hundreds of results.

This isn't working, she thought.

Maybe there was another way to approach the problem.

She closed her eyes and thought hard. What did they know?

They knew that the killer had been contacting Nicky. He had been sending her emails, leaving her riddles, and planting clues. He was taunting her, and it seemed like he was doing it for a reason.

What did it all mean?

She opened her eyes, and an idea began to form in her mind.

What if...

She sat up as she began to type another search term into the database. Someone who was mute, had a criminal record, but also had a tech background. Someone capable of hacking information about Nicky.

She felt a surge of excitement as the results began to filter in.

"It's working!" she said, and Ken looked up.

"What's working?" he asked, and she nodded to the computer.

"Look at that," she said, and he leaned forward. "Looks like we've got a bunch of names..."

"But how many of them match the criteria?" Ken asked, and Nicky shrugged.

"I'm not sure," she said with a sigh. "It's not enough. We have too many names, and we don't have enough information on all of them. We need more. We need more information."

"How do we do that?" Ken asked, and Nicky began to type more.

She had to have thousands of results, but Nicky tried to sift through them, looking for anyone who seemed promising.

Then, finally, she stopped on one. Kevin Finch. According to the database, he was working as a coder for a tech firm in Miami. But they fired him for theft, and he was arrested for attempted burglary from his company. His lawyer claimed he was trying to get his job back, but he ended up in prison. He had a speech impediment--he wasn't mute, but he could still fit the bill, if he was someone who didn't like his own voice.

Plus, most importantly, he was released from prison eight months ago--two months before Delilah went missing. And he moved to Wahoe Bay four months ago.

"Ken, check this guy out," Nicky said.

"Okay," Ken said, looking at a screen. He was silent for several moments as he took in the information. "Shit. He might be our guy."

"The timeline matches up," Nicky said. "And he has a background in tech. If he's really good, he could've hacked databases to find out information about me. He could be the one sending the recordings."

"It's worth looking into," Ken said. "Let's keep digging."

Nicky and Ken continued to look through the database, searching for more information on Kevin Finch. They soon found out that he had been in and out of trouble with the law since he was a teenager, but had never been convicted of anything serious until the attempted burglary. He had a history of minor offenses like possession of marijuana, theft, disorderly conduct, and vandalism. He had attended college for two years before dropping out due to financial hardship, though he still seemed to have a knack for coding and technology in general.

When they looked deeper into Kevin Finch's background, they discovered that he was raised by his single mother in Miami. His father had abandoned them when Kevin was young, leaving his mother to raise him alone with her other child, and barely scraping by on her meager wages from her job as a waitress. Despite this difficult upbringing, Kevin managed to excel academically and even earned high marks in his computer science classes at school.

However, despite his achievements in academics, Kevin seemed to harbor deep resentment towards authority figures in general--particularly those in law enforcement--and he often expressed these feelings through writing angry letters or posting inflammatory comments online. Nicky also noticed that many of these posts had a violent undertone, particularly toward women.

Well, Nicky was a woman, and an FBI agent--someone he could perceive as one of the authority figures he'd always hated. Nicky still wasn't sure why he'd zeroed in on her and sent her the recordings, or why he was playing these games, but either way, it seemed like Kevin was worth looking into.

Nicky got his address from the database. He lived on the outskirts of Wahoe Bay, in a small neighborhood far from the resorts.

"Looks like we found our guy," Ken said. "Do we want to bring him in?"

Nicky nodded, standing up. "Let's go see what he has to say."

CHAPTER NINETEEN

Nicky gripped the steering wheel as she drove down the road that would lead to Kevin's house, along the shoreline of Wahoe Bay. The blue-gray sky glinted with orange and pink hues, the stretching shoreline darkened by slowly approaching night. The salty sea breeze and slight smoky scent of the engine, the tinge of exhaust from other cars and the faint waft of fish filled the car. But Nicky couldn't appreciate the scenery of Wahoe Bay, not when Delilah's life was on the line.

If Kevin was their guy, then they were close.

They hadn't contacted him first; they'd decided to catch him off guard. They didn't know if he was involved with the murders, or if he was the one sending the recordings to Nicky, but they wanted to bring him in for questioning, just to find out what he knew.

At long last, they arrived. The house was a small, one-story structure, and there was a dented old car in the driveway. Nicky parked on the street and they got out, walking up the driveway to the front door as a cool breeze blew from the sea behind. She nodded at Ken, who nodded back.

No matter what happened here, they had to be ready.

Nicky knocked loudly on the door, and waited.

After several moments, there was no answer. She knocked again and waited, but there was still no response.

Nicky frowned, feeling a chill of unease. She knocked a third time, more loudly this time, but still there was no answer. She stepped back and looked at the windows, peering through them to see if there was any sign of life inside. But the house seemed dark and still; it seemed like no one was home.

Nicky glanced back at Ken, her stomach sinking. Maybe they were too late; maybe Kevin had already skipped town. He had been their only lead so far, and if he was gone...

But Nicky refused to give up hope just yet. She would knock one more time and then she'd take a closer look around the property for any signs that he might be hiding out somewhere nearby.

But then, just as she was about to knock again, something happened.

A loud gunshot echoed from inside the house, sending a chill down Nicky's spine. Her heart pounded in her chest as she reached for her gun and drew it out, ready for whatever might come next.

What had happened? Was Kevin inside? Did he know they were here? Or was someone else in there with him? She didn't know, but one thing was certain: the situation had become a lot more dangerous.

Both Ken and Nicky pressed their backs to the wall on either side of the door, their guns drawn. They looked at each other and nodded.

They had to go in.

Ken took a breath then kicked the door with all his strength, and it cracked open, the wood splintering as it flew off its hinges. They rushed in, their guns trained on the darkness within.

The house was dark, but Nicky's eyes quickly adjusted to the dim light of the living room. It was empty, but she could hear movement from further inside; someone had obviously heard them and was trying to hide from them.

Nicky moved slowly, her gun pointed outward--but then, a shot fired from somewhere in the house. Ken dove at her, pulling her to the floor behind the living room couch.

A bullet flew into the window behind them, shattering it.

Someone was shooting from inside the house. But they didn't know where.

Nicky's heart pounded, her adrenaline on high. One wrong move could mean death for both of them.

She and Ken stayed where they were, huddled close on the floor. Nicky scanned the darkness around them, searching for any sign of where the shooter was firing from.

"Who--are--you!" someone shouted, their words broken up. The speech impediment...

This was him. Kevin.

Another gunshot went off and ricocheted through the house. Nicky and Ken ducked lower, grabbing onto each other.

Nicky shot her own gun into the ceiling, bracing herself at the sound. "FBI!" she shouted. "Hold your fire!"

The room went still.

For a moment, nothing happened. Then, they heard the sound of footsteps running away and the back door slamming shut. Whoever had been shooting was gone.

Nicky and Ken got up slowly, their guns still drawn. They cautiously moved through the house, looking for any signs of Kevin or whoever had been shooting at them. But it seemed like they were too late; the shooter had already escaped, and there was no sign of Kevin anywhere in the house.

But then, they heard it. The sound of a car engine starting up outside.

Nicky and Ken rushed out the front door, ready to follow whoever had been inside the house. Sure enough, they saw Kevin's car speeding away down the street, and without wasting any time, they ran after it.

The chase was on.

Nicky dove at the rental car and hopped behind the wheel, with Ken swiftly sliding into the passenger side. He knew by now that Nicky was always the driver--considering she'd been kidnapped by a man in his van when she was a teenager, she had never grown comfortable relinquishing control of the wheel.

And unfortunately for Kevin, that made Nicky one hell of a driver.

She pressed the pedal to the floor, and the car roared to life as they sped off after him. The engine grumbled as they sped through the streets of Wahoe Bay, weaving in and out of traffic. Kevin was still several car lengths ahead, but she had no intention of letting him get away.

They drove for what felt like an eternity, their cars careening around corners and whipping past palm trees. Nicky's grip on the wheel was tight as her knuckles turned white; Ken held onto the side door handle to keep from being thrown around in his seat.

Nicky kept her focus on the road ahead; she had no time for distractions if she wanted to catch up to Kevin. She could feel Ken clutching onto his seatbelt with a white-knuckled grip as she navigated the tight turns and sharp curves of the winding roads.

Finally, after what seemed like hours, Nicky spotted Kevin's car up ahead--and it was heading straight for a boat dockside! She pushed down harder on the gas pedal and closed in on him until she was almost side-by-side with his vehicle.

Kevin rolled down his window, and panic slammed into Nicky's chest as she saw him point his gun at them. She swerved away as he fired a gun, missing the car.

"So, it's gonna be like that," she said, clenching her teeth.

She didn't want to ruin this rental car, but she would if she had to.

"Careful, Lyons," Ken said, "this guy is a maniac."

Up ahead, she could see Kevin's car weaving crazily through the docks. He was clearly trying to lose them, and he was almost succeeding.

But Nicky wasn't going to let him.

She grabbed the wheel with both hands and pushed it to the side. The car skidded, swerving right as it began to speed off the road and down to the docks.

And that's when she saw it: the large, metal shipping container directly in the path of the car. She had to make a split-second decision.

She turned the wheel to the left, pulling hard to avoid smashing into the container. The car slid off the road and onto the grass below, flying past the shipping container and landing with a thud at the edge of the docks.

The car skidded to a stop, smoke billowing from the engine. Nicky and Ken both leapt out of the car and onto the sand, their guns pointed at the car, but Kevin had already fled. It was dark now, night settling over the beach, and civilians looked on from the town.

Then, up the beach, she saw him.

Kevin.

He was running on foot.

Nicky and Ken were off like a shot, sprinting down the beach after Kevin. The two of them worked together to close in on him, their footsteps echoing in the night. They could hear his heavy breathing as they neared closer and closer, but he was still several yards ahead of them.

They ran up the beach, their feet pounding against the sand. Nicky felt the wind in her hair as she pushed herself to go faster and faster. Kevin was fast, but she knew that if they kept pushing themselves, they would eventually catch up to him.

The two of them ran until their lungs were burning from exhaustion. They were close now, and Kevin was losing steam.

Soon enough, they had him surrounded.

Kevin looked around frantically, his whole body heaving. He was trying to keep his feet running, but he was slowing down.

"Stop running," Nicky said, her gun still raised. "You can't run forever."

Kevin stopped in his tracks, his chest heaving. Finally, he thew his hands up in surrender. Ken and Nicky continued to walk toward him.

"Come on," Nicky said, her gun still pointed at him. "Turn around, flat on your stomach, hands behind your head."

Kevin did as he was told, his body trembling. Nicky and Ken cuffed him, and with his hands behind his back, they easily lifted him onto his feet.

He refused to look at them, no matter how hard Nicky tried to meet his eyes. He just averted her stare. She couldn't help the anger that coursed through her as she got a close look at his face. He had short black hair and pock marks on his cheeks, his eyes as dark as coal. He looked like a guilty child now, and not a criminal who'd just shot at them and caused them to race through Wahoe Bay, endangering citizens and property.

Most importantly, he could be the one who had Delilah. Who killed June.

"Well, Kevin?" Nicky asked. "You know why we chased you, don't you?"

He sulked away. "I... I--do..."

"Good," Ken said, crossing his arms, "then you won't mind coming down to the station with us."

CHAPTER TWENTY

Nicky squinted bright lights at the Bahamas police station as she and Ken led Kevin into the interrogation room. They had finally caught up to him, and they'd brought him into the station directly. He didn't say much on the drive--but Nicky had a feeling he would be talking soon.

He looked at the ground as they led him into the room, his hands cuffed in front of him. As soon as he entered the room, he dropped into a chair, his face sullen.

For a moment, there was silence. Nicky and Ken stood by the door, waiting for o start.

"All right," Nicky said, crossing her arms. "Tell me where she is."

Kevin looked up. Wordlessly, he shook his head. Then, he managed, "She?"

"Don't bullshit me." Nicky went over to the table and sat down, leaning her elbows forward. "I know who you are. I know why you're here. I know what you did to June, and I know what you did to Delilah."

His eyes widened as she said her name. He stared at Nicky, and she stared right back at him. Finally, he spoke.

"I... I didn't do anything to..." he said.

She glanced back at Ken, who sighed and sat down next to her. Now facing off against Kevin, they both had their work cut out for them. With his speech impediment, Kevin was definitely not much of a talker, but they needed him to confess.

Because the more Nicky looked at him, the more guilty he became in her eyes.

He fit the profile perfectly. A loner with a criminal record. Speech issues. Someone who didn't have their own voice, so they were using the voices of others.

He could easily be the one who had sent Nicky the recordings. If he was, then he already knew who she was.

She decided to tug on that thread, to gauge his reactions.

"Kevin, you already know who I am, don't you?" Nicky said.

He looked at her with big, guilty eyes, then shook his head.

"You do," Nicky said. "You've been sending me recordings. Recordings of the women you've been holding hostage."

Kevin frowned at that, then shook his head rapidly. "No--I have--no--women?"

Nicky's eyes narrowed. "You've been sending me recordings, Kevin."

"I--no," he said again, a little more desperately this time. "I--didn't do--anything!"

Nicky looked back at Ken. He nodded, then leaned further in towards Kevin.

"Look," Ken said. "We can either keep going around in circles here, or you can tell us what you know about Delilah and June."

Kevin shook his head again, but his face had gone pale now. He opened his mouth to speak, but nothing came out. It was clear that he wanted to say something--but he didn't want to admit anything either. His fear was palpable in the room; Nicky could feel it coming off of him like a wave of heat.

Finally, after what felt like an eternity of silence, he spoke up again.

"I... I don't know anything," he said finally in a small voice. "I swear I don't."

Nicky watched him carefully for any signs of deception, but all she saw was fear and confusion on his face.

"I swear," Kevin said, his voice trembling. "I had nothing to do with any of this--I don't know who Delilah is."

He looked away and rubbed his forehead, but Nicky could tell he was lying. He just didn't want to admit it, which meant she needed to find another way to get him talking.

She took a deep breath and tried again.

"Okay," she said softly. "Let's start from the beginning then. Tell me what you're doing in Wahoe Bay. You moved here from Miami, correct?"

Kevin nodded. "My--brother's--house."

Nicky paused. Kevin's sibling--that was mentioned in his file. In their hurry to get to him, she had overlooked the detail that Kevin's brother might live here in Wahoe Bay. She nodded at Ken, a silent request for him to confirm Kevin was telling the truth. Ken took out his phone and checked the information, then shot her a nod. So, it was Kevin's brother's house. Nicky focused on Kevin.

"You have quite the criminal record," Nicky said. "You were arrested for stealing from the company you worked at, and it seems you struggle to listen to authority."

She saw his cheeks flush, his face drop. "I... I do... but I wasn't doing anything wrong."

"You stole money from your company," Ken said. "That's wrong."

Kevin just shook his head, his eyes welling with tears. "I never meant to hurt anyone. I just--I wanted to help my brother, and I wanted to help my mom..."

"So you stole," Ken said, crossing his arms. "And your mother was sick?"

Kevin nodded. "Yeah... she is... but... but I never hurt anyone--"

"You hurt June Peterson," Nicky said. "Didn't you, Kevin?"

Kevin shook his head quickly, adamantly denying the accusation. "No--I-I didn't hurt anyone! I never touched any of those women--"

"But you were somehow involved," Nicky said, her voice firm. "You were sending recordings... How did you end up with them?"

Kevin looked away, his face pale and full of fear. He was clearly scared to admit anything, but Nicky had a feeling she knew what he was hiding. She leaned forward and looked him in the eyes.

"Come on now," she said softly. "We know you have something to do with this. So either tell us what happened or we'll have no choice but to keep this going all night. I don't believe for a second you would shoot at us, then run away in your car if you weren't hiding something. So what is it, Kevin?"

Kevin stared at her for a few moments, his eyes wide with fear. He was clearly terrified, and Nicky could practically see the wheels turning in his head as he frantically searched for an answer that would keep him out of trouble. But then, all of a sudden, his face went blank and he simply stopped talking. His lips were closed tight and he refused to look at either of them, as if he had resigned himself to the fact that they would never get an explanation from him.

Ken stared at Kevin, his gaze intense as if trying to make Kevin talk through sheer force of will. But still Kevin said nothing, just stared ahead with a haunted expression on his face. He seemed paralyzed with fear, refusing to speak or even look at them. Nicky sighed and leaned back, disappointed that he wasn't willing to cooperate. She had hoped talking would get him to open up and reveal what he was hiding, but it seemed she had pushed too hard.

Just then, an officer came into the room, an urgent look on his face. With the door opened, Nicky could hear some commotion coming from inside the police station.

"Agents, there's a guy here demanding to see the suspect," the officer said.

"Who is he?" Nicky asked, frowning.

"He says he's Kevin's brother."

Nicky and Ken exchanged a look before getting to their feet.

The three of them rushed down the hall, following the officer towards a back room. As they entered, Nicky saw a man who looked a lot like Kevin standing in the center of the room, shouting at officers to let him past.

"Hey!" Nicky shouted, and the room went quiet, looking over at them. Even Kevin's brother went quiet, although there was rage all over his face.

"You," he said. "You're the ones who took my brother."

"What are you doing here?" Ken asked him gruffly.

"I'm here for my brother," he said sternly, his gaze never leaving Nicky or Ken's faces. "He needs help, and I'm not going to let him rot in here alone because of you bastards."

Nicky glanced around the room at the faces of the other officers, who looked on apprehensively, as though unsure what else to do.

Nicky sighed. She wanted to interrogate Kevin more--but surely, if Kevin was guilty, then his brother had to be involved too.

"Come this way, Mr. Finch," Nicky said, "and we can talk in private."

"It's Jerry," he cut in, "and you need to take me to my brother now."

"We'll talk to you alone first," Ken said sternly.

Jerry glared at them for a few moments, then nodded. He followed Nicky and Ken out of the room, and they soon found themselves in a small, private office.

They each took a seat, and Jerry sat across from them. He was still bristling with anger, but he seemed to be willing to listen now.

"I don't care what you think my brother did," he said firmly. "He's not capable of doing something like this."

"Your brother shot at us and then fled from us," Nicky fired back. "He's guilty of something, and I think you know that."

"If he shot at you," Jerry said, "then that was probably just a reaction. He was scared, because of you people. You ambushed him while he was home, and you scared him into running. You didn't give him a chance to explain anything."

"And what do you think he was going to explain?" Nicky asked.

"I don't know!" Jerry exclaimed. He looked away and sighed. Suddenly, his anger melted away, and it was guilt that took over his face. "Just... let my brother go, damn it. Take me instead."

Nicky leaned forward, her pulse racing. Was Jerry about to admit to something? Take credit for the crime?

"What would we take you for?" Nicky asked.

Jerry sighed. "The drugs, okay? They're mine. They're not Kevin's. He was just trying to protect me. He knows what's at stake for me, that's why he shot at you. I guarantee it."

Nicky exchanged a look with Ken. This wasn't going in the direction she thought it would.

"What drugs?" Nicky asked.

Jerry shifted in his seat, looking uncomfortable. "Cocaine," he said finally. "We've been selling it on the street for a while now. Kevin was just helping me out."

Nicky nodded, understanding what was going on now. Jerry had been using Kevin to cover up his own criminal activity, and Kevin had taken the fall for him. That was why he hadn't wanted to talk when they first met him at his house--he knew that admitting anything would get both of them into trouble.

But this could be a ruse. A coverup for what they were really doing.

"No, Jerry," Nicky said, "Kevin was arrested on suspicion of murdering June Peterson and holding another woman, Delilah Roberts, hostage."

"What?" Jerry exclaimed. He shook his head. "No, that's not true! We wouldn't do something like that--we're just drug dealers. That's it. I swear to you, we have nothing to do with those crimes. Go ahead, search my whole house, you're gonna find drugs, but nothing to do with any women."

Nicky paused, considering that maybe, Jerry was telling the truth. If they searched his place and found no trace of Delilah, or anything linking them to the recordings or June's death... then they would be in the clear.

And if that were the case, then they were wasting precious time. Time that could be life or death for Delilah.

The thought made Nicky's stomach cinch with anxiety. The fear of failure suddenly came back, more real and tangible than ever before. It was getting late, and Delilah was out there... she needed their help. Now.

"Okay," she said, "we'll check your story out. But if you're lying to us and we find out, you won't be able to lie your way out of jail time. Wait here."

Jerry nodded gravely, his face still pale with fear. He watched as Nicky and Ken walked out of the room without another word.

Once alone in the hallway, Nicky turned to Ken, who wore a thoughtful expression.

"What do you make of his story?" Ken asked.

"It could be legit," Nicky said. "We need to get a team over there to gut their house now and confirm. If they are innocent, then we're wasting time here."

Ken nodded. "I agree. Let's get them on the move."

Ken went to walk away. But something in Nicky wanted to stop him--the sudden need for comfort. For a reminder that they could do this, and not fail.

"Wait," Nicky said, grabbing him by the arm. She hesitated, only for a moment, not quite knowing what she was going to say. "Sorry, I'm just... do you really still believe we can do this?"

Ken looked at her for a long moment, his gaze serious and intent. "Of course, Nicky," he said. "I believe in us. I believe in you."

A warmth rushed through Nicky, and she felt an urge she didn't quite understand. A need she didn't quite know how to express.

Her confidence returned, and she nodded.

"Let's get moving," she said. "We can do this."

Ken smiled at her, and she felt like she could keep going with that alone.

"We can do this," he agreed.

CHAPTER TWENTY ONE

Delilah woke up, groggy, in the back of the car. She felt like hell. Her head was spinning and her neck ached and the car was moving, but she didn't know where.

She had no idea, for the moment, where she was going, or what she was doing. As the car drove through the streets, her mind slowly started to become clear, and after a few minutes, she remembered everything.

He had left her here.

Her kidnapper had left her, bound and gagged in the back of his car, a piece of duct tape over her mouth so she couldn't make a sound. She could barely move, with her body all tied up, but through the window of the car, it looked like a building was beside her.

But she was out. Out of his damn basement. Could she reach someone? Maybe someone would walk by, and she could kick at the window?

She didn't know what to do. He would kill her soon, she was sure of it. He'd killed that other poor woman, and it was only a matter of time before Delilah was next.

She wasn't going to have a chance. She was only going to be able to escape for a moment.

She started to cry again, but what was the point? No one was going to hear her, and no one was going to help her.

Her tears slowly rolled down her cheeks. She was crying more out of frustration than anything else.

It was all over.

She wanted to say she wasn't scared. She wanted to say she wasn't going to be some sobbing mess in the back of the car, crying as she waited to die.

But she was scared.

She was very scared.

She had accepted it would happen, but it was the kind of thing that was easier to accept when it was theoretical. It was easier to accept when it was some other woman that wasn't her, who she didn't know, and who she didn't love.

Now it was happening, and it was all too real, and it was all too terrifying.

She didn't know what to do. She didn't know how to escape. She didn't know what was going to happen to her.

She was a crying mess in the back of the car. She was sobbing uncontrollably, and she could feel the tears streaming down her face.

She missed her life. She had taken it for granted. The small acting gigs she did as a kid, and even her voice work--she had dreamed of becoming a star, but not like this.

She thought of her life in Miami. All the auditions she'd done, the way her mother had tried to prop her up like an item to be sold.

She thought of her friends, and the way they had all moved onto new things, new relationships, new jobs, new cities.

She thought of her old life, and she thought that she had been happy, for all that it wasn't perfect.

She didn't want to die.

She was crying so much, she was a sobbing mess in the back of the car. She didn't care who she looked like. She didn't care what anyone would think of her if they saw her like this. She was just a girl, begging for her life.

Please, someone… please help me.

She was still tied up, and gagged, but the tape over her mouth was loosening. She tried to scream through the duct tape, but it was muffled. She was going to die anyway, so what did it matter?

Please... someone... please... help me.

She'd been so desperate to be a star, and now it was all over.

He was going to throw her body into the sea.

She would never see her mother again.

She would never kiss anyone again.

She would never get to live again.

She would never get to exist again.

He was going to kill her, and there was nothing she could do but wait.

Was anyone even looking for her? Probably not. Delilah was a nobody--no one would remember her, and no one was looking for her.

Her kidnapper had never spoke. She had never heard his voice. She wasn't even sure if he had one.

e had always just been a black shadow in a dark basement.

He was going to kill her. He was going to take everything from her.

She thought about calling out for help. She thought about screaming.

But why would she?

It was useless.

But she did it anyway.

She screamed as loud as she could through the duct tape over her mouth.

She screamed for help.

She screamed for mercy.

She screamed for anyone to save her.

But no one came.

She screamed and screamed until her throat hurt. She screamed for anybody, anybody at all to save her, to let her out of the car, to help her.

But no one came.

She screamed and screamed, but nobody came to save her. They couldn't hear her muffled screams.

She didn't know where he went. It seemed like maybe he was looking for another woman to take home. And maybe then, once he found Delilah's replacement, he'd just kill her like he did to June.

She tried to calm down. She tried to slow down her breathing, but she couldn't. She was shaking, and crying, and she could hardly stand it.

And then she heard a sound.

A siren.

She heard a siren, and she knew what it meant.

There was a police car out there somewhere.

Delilah started making noise again and attempted to kick the car. But the sound of the siren faded away, taking her hope with it.

She didn't know what to do. She started to cry again.

She just wanted to get out of the car. She wanted to run away from this maniac. She wanted to get away from the car, and to make a break for it.

But how could she? She was tied up, and she was in the back of the car.

There was no way out.

Delilah started to cry again. She slumped down in the car, sobbing quietly, waiting for whatever was going to happen.

No one was coming to save her.

CHAPTER TWENTY TWO

Back at the hotel room, Nicky sat at the table with Ken, trying to think of their next move--but her mind was drawing a blank. Outside the windows, the sky was dark, the stars twinkling off the sea surrounding the Bahamas. A calm whoosh came in through the windows, and yet the turmoil in Nicky's mind wouldn't let her breathe.

They had their laptops open and had been trying to find more viable suspects, but nothing had come up yet. After a raid of Jerry and Kevin's house, it had been determined that they had drugs--but no evidence to suggest they had anything to do with Delilah's disappearance or June's murder.

Nicky was tired, restless, and she needed a shower, but she couldn't allow herself to relax. She knew she wouldn't be able to sleep anyway.

Nicky sighed and checked her phone. She still hadn't heard back from her contact at the prison regarding whatever Fred Garrison seemed to know. She bit her lip and checked her texts, only to see, once again, no message.

She sent another one: *Anything?*

She figured she'd probably have to go in person to talk to Garrison. The idea of finding more about the man who'd kidnapped her and Rosie seemed closer than ever, and yet still so impossibly far.

That event was the reason why Nicky was where she was today. Why she cared so much about saving Delilah's life. Why she became an FBI agent, and while only in her late-twenties, she knew she was going to dedicate the rest of her life to this job.

Those three days she'd spent trapped in that lake house haunted her. Three days trapped by a madman with her sister ten years ago.

In many ways, Nicky knew she'd never get over it. Her psychiatrist, Dr. Graham, had diagnosed her with survivor's guilt.

Nicky had heard the term before, but didn't know it applied to her until her sessions with Graham. She was afraid to fall asleep, afraid to close her eyes because she would see Rosie's face.

"Nicky," Ken said.

She shook herself out of her thoughts and looked at him.

"What?"

"Is this case getting to you?" he asked.

Nicky blinked. "What do you mean?"

"I don't know. You seem more stressed than usual." His face reddened as he rubbed the back of his neck. "Don't get me wrong, I like that you came to me for comfort earlier... it just... wasn't like you."

Nicky's chest warmed. She knew it wasn't like her. Romantic relationships weren't her specialty, but she wanted to be more open with Ken. She wanted to get there with him. He wasn't just her partner at the FBI anymore--they were something more, even if they hadn't kissed yet.

"It is getting to me," Nicky admitted. "I feel like I'm running in circles. I feel like I'm not going to be able to get closure with Delilah. Like I'll never be able to stop being scared that I'll get kidnapped again, or worse. That I'll never be able to finish this job." She clenched her fists, her nails digging into her palms. "And I feel like I'm the only one who can't see that."

Ken stared at her for a long moment, his eyes shimmering in the light of the laptop. "I know," he finally said. "But we have to be patient."

Nicky shook her head. "I don't know what else there is to do. We've searched every name, every person of interest, and we've found nothing. We've gone over everything multiple times. What else is there to do?"

"We keep at it," Ken said quietly. "So we can save Delilah, and we can make sure that this guy can't do anything to anyone else. You know we're going to find something."

Nicky nodded, but she wasn't sure. She felt like this case was leading down a dead end, and she was running out of time.

"I hope so," she said. "I'm not sure what else we can do."

Ken sighed. "I know," he said. "But I promise we'll find something. I won't stop until I know this guy can't hurt anyone else."

Nicky looked at him. "But I can't shake the feeling that this is going to be the end of the task force. If we lose Delilah, then I don't think I can, in good conscience, continue as the leader. We've lost too many girls."

Stressed crossed Ken's brow, and he sighed. He leaned forward and grabbed her hands across the table. She melted into the warm feeling of his rough hands on hers. "Those losses are on my conscience too, Nicky," he said, his voice low. "This isn't all on you. You're not alone."

Nicky nodded. "I know. But I'm the one leading this investigation." She pulled her hands away from him and rubbed them over her face. "I should have found something by now."

Ken stood up. "We will," he said. "I promise you."

Nicky looked at him. "How can you be so sure?"

Ken took a deep breath and looked out the window, his gaze faraway. "Because it's us. We always figure it out. Isn't that true?"

Nicky appreciated the sentiment, and in many ways, they did always figure it out. But not always without losses. Still, it was sweet of Ken to try and make Nicky feel better. She appreciated that more than he knew.

"Thank you," Nicky said, her voice soft. "For being here and for believing in me."

Ken smiled and nodded. "I'm always here for you," he said.

Nicky returned the smile, relief washing over her. She knew that Ken had her back, no matter what happened. His presence was a reminder that she wasn't alone in this fight--she had him with her every step of the way. She felt more determined than ever to keep going, to find Delilah and make sure that this monster was brought to justice once and for all.

"You're right," she said quietly. "I just wish we were closer to the answer."

Ken smiled. "We will be," he said confidently. Then, he stepped around the table and pulled her into a hug. Nicky felt safe in his arms, like nothing else in the world mattered. She wanted to stay there forever; it was exactly what she needed at that moment.

She looked up at him and smiled gratefully. "Thank you," she said softly. "For being here with me."

Ken smiled back, his eyes twinkling with understanding and compassion before he leaned down and gave her a gentle kiss on the forehead.

"Of course," he said softly, brushing her hair away from her face before stepping back and taking her hand again. Nicky felt a wave of warmth wash over her as they stood together in companionable silence for a few moments before they both turned back to their work, feeling more determined than ever to find what they were looking for so they could bring Delilah home safely and stop this criminal once and for all. It was these moments that made Nicky truly thankful for having Ken by her side in such a trying time, and it was these moments that helped Nicky keep pushing forward despite the darkness of the situation.

Refocusing on work, Nicky stared at her laptop and tried to think if there was anything else she could be missing. Any other thread to pull, or an angle to run down she hadn't thought of yet.

She had to look at the facts they did have. The killer had taken Delilah and murdered June. He also somehow knew Nicky's personal information, enough to deliver the first recording to her apartment, and the second to her phone.

June hadn't been missing for long before she was murdered, but Delilah had been missing for six months.

It seemed like his timeline was escalating...

Was it possible he had taken another victim already?

At that moment, a thought struck Nicky.

They had spent so much time looking for the killer--but what if they looked for another victim? If they could identify someone else who was potentially taken by him, or a target of him, then maybe it would lead them to him.

Nicky didn't buy for a second this would end with June and Delilah. No--there would be another victim. She was sure of it.

"Ken," Nicky said, "what if instead of profiling a suspect, we profile another victim?"

He frowned. "What do you mean?"

"I mean, this guy has a type," Nicky said. "Delilah did voice work and was a great singer. And so was June. She was a musician. They also both had ginger hair, which seems to be pretty rare for the locals here. I haven't seen many people with red hair."

"Now that you mention it, I guess that's true," Ken said. "So what are you thinking?"

"Let's see if there are any other young redhead musicians or voice talents in Wahoe Bay," Nicky said. "They could be potential targets."

"Or they could be completely unrelated," Ken said. "I mean, if the killer is targeting redheads, it's not like they have to be voice actors."

Nicky sighed. "I know that. But it's a lead, right? It's somewhere to look. It's a place to start."

"Yeah, it is," Ken agreed. "But it's not going to be easy to find them all, especially since we don't know where to begin."

"I know," Nicky said. "But maybe there's a way to narrow it down. Come on." She turned to her laptop and got to work. "We need to at least try."

Nicky started by searching through the town's public records, looking for any young women with red hair who had a history of music or vocal performance. After searching through countless names and addresses, she narrowed it down to fifteen potential targets. She then looked up each one in the police database, cross-referencing their information with any criminal activity or missing person reports from the past six months.

One name immediately caught her eye: Alicia O'Connor. According to the database, Alicia was a twenty-six year old vocal student at Wahoe Bay College. And she was a natural redhead, like June and Delilah.

"I have one," Ken said, as if on cue.

Nicky nodded. "Me too. Alicia O'Conner. Twenty-six, natural redhead, and a vocal student."

"Mine's Karen Whittaker, also a natural redhead, twenty-one, and a street performer. She moved here two years ago."

Nicky looked up in surprise. "Really? That's great work, Ken."

"Thanks," he said. "Now what?"

Nicky glanced at the clock. It was getting late. "We should split up," she said. "We'll cover more ground that way. You take Karen, I'll take Alicia."

Ken nodded. "Sounds good. Let's see what we can find."

"Yeah," Nicky said, her heart pounding in her chest. "Let's do this." She looked at Ken one more time, her eyes shining.

She had a good feeling about this. It put Nicky at ease to know that they were finally making some kind of progress and that they were that much closer to bringing Delilah home and stopping the killer before he could hurt anyone else.

They could still get some answers before it was too late.

CHAPTER TWENTY THREE

He peered at her through the window of her home, mesmerized by her fiery red hair as she made dinner for herself, humming along to the tune on her radio. It was warm in there, calm lights shimmering off the photos on her wall.

He was happy to learn she lived alone.

She seemed like the kind of girl who could come and go as she pleased, with no burdens to tie her down. He wondered if she had a boyfriend, if anyone would be at her house that night. If anyone would come to interrupt them.

It was worth the risk. *She* was worth the risk. Her natural red hair was stunning, like a flame. Like his mother's.

As he watched her pour oil onto a pan, he remembered the meals his mother used to make him.

Even though she was gone, he could still smell the delicious aroma of her cooking. He remembered how she would hum along to the radio as she prepared the food.

He wondered if his mother had ever felt lonely before she died.

He remembered the way she used to pat the back of his head, the way she used to smile and laugh at his jokes. He remembered the way she used to sing, the way he used to lie in bed for hours at night, amazed by the sound.

He remembered the way she used to wave goodbye to him every morning, the way she used to tell him to be safe as she dropped him off at school. He remembered the way she used to hug him before his trips, the way she used to cry as he left. He remembered the way she used to hold him as she got sicker, the way she used to squeeze his hand as the rain poured outside. He remembered the way she used to say "I love you" before she passed, the way she used to tell him to keep going.

He thought of his mother and felt a deep sense of love and admiration. He wanted to be the kind of person his mother was, strong and determined despite the odds. He wanted to make her proud, even if she wasn't here physically. She'd always taught him to fight for his voice.

And he would do just that.

He stared at the girl in the window, humming along to the music on her radio, her whole demeanor so peaceful as she cooked her dinner.

His mother had been his voice, but at the end of her life, when the sickness took over, not even she would be listened to.

Still, he held such fond memories of her. She was the only one who ever truly loved him. Who heard him.

He thought of all those silent drives between them, when she'd hum along to the radio. He could never make a noise, although he'd desperately wished he could.

He remembered the way he'd stare out of the window, watching the world pass by. He'd wonder what it would be like to have a voice, to be able to speak and share his thoughts with someone.

He took one last look at the girl in the window before turning away, feeling as if he had been given a sign from his mother that everything was going to be okay.

He wanted to tell the girl in the window that, that he could feel his mother's love from so far away. He wanted to thank her for reminding him of his mother, for making him feel close to her again. She ignited something deeper in him than Delilah ever did.

It had been ten years since his mother died, and he still didn't have his voice. People ignored him on the street. He was never seen. Never able to property communicate. Most people didn't speak sign language, and they didn't care to learn. The older he got, the less people cared about him.

But what do people care about? Missing girls. He'd learned that. Especially if they were privileged and pretty. Enough for even the FBI to give a damn what happened to them.

That was what had initially drawn his eye to the idea of taking one for his own.

A new voice.

He'd heard Delilah on a TV show and learned she lived in Miami. She had seemed perfect. But the longer he held her, the less it seemed like the world cared about finding her.

Then he saw the news. About the vice president's daughter, and that FBI agent--Nicky Lyons.

A woman who had such a strong voice that all around her listened.

He had been formulating his plan ever since--a plan to get her attention and make her listen, once and for all. He would make the world listen.

June's body had been found--he heard about it on the news. Along with it, reports that two unnamed FBI agents were in Wahoe Bay, attempting to solve the crime.

Nicky was here. She'd followed his clues. He had a feeling she was smart enough to figure it out.

And so he needed his perfect voice. Delilah's was no good to him anymore.

He looked back into the house, at the red-haired woman, still arranging her meal.

He didn't want to scare her.

But he couldn't wait any longer.

She carried her plate of food into her dining room, setting it down on her kitchen table. He snuck around the back. He would have to strike when she least expected it--then he would take her. Make her his new voice.

And then, he could finally kill Delilah.

CHAPTER TWENTY FOUR

Ken could feel a headache forming in his temples as he drove up to Karen Whittaker's home. It was getting late into the night, after nine p.m., and they'd been at this for so long that his skull was pounding. He wasn't sure if Nicky's lead was sound; if checking in on these random, red-headed women would lead them anywhere, but he had to have faith in her.

Truthfully, she needed it.

Ken had gotten another rental car, and it was almost strange to drive himself while on the job, considering Nicky never let him take the wheel. He respected it, and it was nice to be a passenger, but sometimes it did add to the feeling that this was Nicky's story, and he was only along for the red.

As Ken approached Karen's house, he couldn't help but reminiscence over the past several months he'd been partnered with Nicky Lyons at the FBI.

It felt like a lifetime ago that he'd been vying for her spot, that he felt outshined by her, when she was so much younger than him. Ken was thirty-five, and Nicky hadn't even turned thirty yet.

But then he got to know her. And see her heart, and her passion, and her unending work ethic.

Nicky deserved to be the head of this team, and he was damn glad he got to be by her side for it all.

He hadn't felt any kind of real love for a woman since high school, when his girlfriend was murdered, and he wasn't there to protect her.

He'd always beaten himself up over that. Sure, it was nearly two decades ago, but the pain was still there, embedded into his very being. He'd had flings with women over the years, but never a long-lasting, real relationship.

But Nicky, she was different. She had changed things for him. He wanted them to give it a try, a real try, and make their relationship work.

He'd been so nervous to ask her out, but as soon as he did, it was like a wave of relief had come over him. She said yes, and for the first time in a long time, Ken felt hopeful about his potential romance with Nicky.

Thinking about what had happened to his high school girlfriend still messed with his head. He'd been to therapy about it here and there, but mostly, he'd learned to keep it all bottled up. But a huge part of him had feared getting close to a woman for so many years because he felt like he could just lose her all over again.

He didn't want to feel that way again. He wanted to be able to trust, and love, and open himself up completely to another person. But a part of him was still scared.

Scared of what could happen if he let himself get too close. Scared of the idea that he would be vulnerable again and at the mercy of someone else's actions towards him. It was a fear he had kept locked away for so long, but it was there, and it had been brought back up with Nicky's arrival in his life.

He knew that for them to have any chance at being together, he needed to confront this fear head-on, but it was easier said than done. He'd need time - time to get used to the idea of trusting someone with his heart once more; time to learn how not to be scared about falling in love again.

He was going to dive in head-first with her anyway, and he knew she'd understand that he wanted to take it slow too. They were both in the same place.

He just hoped she was right about this case.

Ken stopped the car outside an ocean-blue house with a curved roof and white shutters on the windows. The architecture was typical of the Bahamas, with its bright colors and tropical motifs giving it a beachy feel. The house was surrounded by lush greenery, giving it an inviting and peaceful atmosphere.

The lights were on, and there was a car in the driveway. Ken sighed, staring at the house, wondering if he should even bother to go up.

Everything was almost certainly fine here, and nothing seemed amiss. But he had told Nicky he'd check, so he got out of the car, stepping into the warm night.

He took a deep breath, steadying himself as he made his way up to the door. He could hear the faint sound of music coming from inside and he hesitated for just a moment before he knocked.

The sound of the knock echoed through the night, but there was no answer. He knocked again, louder this time, and waited.

Still nothing. No one answered the door, and Ken grew worried. His heart started to race as he imagined all sorts of terrible possibilities. What if something had happened to Karen? What if Nicky had been right?

He stepped back, taking another look around the house to see if he could spot anything that might explain why no one was answering. But all he saw were the curtains drawn on each of the windows and a single light glowing from within one of them.

Just as he was about to turn around and leave, he heard the sound of footsteps coming from inside. He took a deep breath, preparing himself for whatever might come next.

The door opened and Karen Whittaker stood there, looking surprised to see him. She blinked a few times, her red hair cascading down her shoulders in gentle waves and her green eyes bright with curiosity. She wore an off-shoulder white dress that flowed down to her feet and she had a set of bangles around each wrist that jingled softly as she moved.

"Can I help you?" she asked, her voice soft but strong.

She was fine.

Ken let out a sigh, slightly embarrassed. He flashed his FBI badge and said, "Evening, ma'am, sorry to bother you so late..."

Karen's brows pinched in concern. "Is everything okay?"

"Yes, it's just..." He sighed. He had to explain it, just in case she could still be a target. "We have reason to believe young women with red hair, who also have musical or voice talent, might be being targeted by a dangerous man in Wahoe Bay. It's not to say we think he's coming after you, but we wanted to inform women matching that description to put up extra security measures. Make sure you lock your door, and don't let anyone you don't know in your home."

Karen's mouth dropped open in shock. "Goodness, that's awful! I had no idea." She shook her head, her expression grave. "Thank you for coming by to tell me this. I'll definitely be taking extra precautions from now on."

"Just for the time being," Ken said. "We're sure we'll find him soon, and then there won't be anything to worry about."

Karen nodded, her expression still serious. "Thank you for coming all the way out here to let me know. I really appreciate it."

She stepped aside to let him out and closed the door behind him. Ken walked back to his car feeling a little bit better, knowing that

Karen was safe and sound. He had done what he was supposed to do and hopefully made a difference in the process.

Either way, Karen was fine--so she wasn't a victim, at least not yet.

He had to let Nicky know.

***

Nicky's pulled her car outside of Alicia O'Conner's house, parking at the side of the road. Her heart was pounding as she thought about what she might find here. Would this be yet another dead end? Would Alicia be okay? Or would this be the last piece of the puzzle that would lead Nicky to Delilah?

Nicky hoped it would be the latter.

After all of this, she couldn't stand another failure. She was sure it would nearly kill her if she couldn't save Delilah.

Maybe this was a shot in the dark, but she had to try. It was all she had.

Just as she was about to get out of the car, her phone rang.

Ken.

Nicky answered it right away. "Ken, what's going on?"

"Hey," his voice said through the phone. "I was just at Karen's. She's fine."

Nicky melted into the seat, relieved. Good. Karen was safe.

But maybe Alicia was the target.

"Okay, good," Nicky said. "I just go to Alicia's. I'm gonna go check it out. Hopefully she's fine too."

"Good luck," Ken said. His voice was deep and full of understanding. He knew how important this mission was to Nicky, and he wanted her to succeed. "I know you can do it."

Nicky smiled, the warmth from Ken's words radiating through her. She felt so much better knowing that he had her back no matter what happened.

"Thanks," she said, feeling a bit more confident with each passing second. "I'm gonna need all the luck I can get."

She hung up the phone and took a deep breath. She stepped out of the car, determination setting in as she approached Alicia's house. She had to do this. No matter what happened tonight, she had to find Delilah and bring her home safely.

Alicia's house gave off a warm aura--Nicky could see the lights were on inside, and she thought she smelled cooking pasta.

She tried to calm herself, to remind herself that Alicia was probably fine. She prayed the woman was okay, but at the same time, she also hoped this could somehow lead her to the killer. Because she needed something, anything, to put her on the right track.

So Nicky knocked on Alicia's door, her heart racing as she waited for a response. But there was no answer.

She knocked again, this time a bit more insistent. She could feel her heart pounding in her chest as she waited for the door to open. But still nothing.

Maybe Alicia was away or asleep.

She knocked again, this time a bit harder. She was determined to get an answer, and she knew that if Alicia was in danger then time was of the essence.

Still, no one answered.

Nicky stepped back from the door, feeling a wave of panic wash over her. What if something had happened to Alicia? What if the killer had already gotten to her?

Just then, the sound of shattering glass. Nicky's stomach dropped. What was--

More glass.

A woman's scream.

Every atom in Nicky's body was shocked to life. She looked through the window, only to see there was another broken window at the back of the house.

And inside, through the archway to the dining room, Nicky saw it.

A red-haired woman--Alicia--fighting off a man in a black hoodie.

CHAPTER TWENTY FIVE

Nicky didn't hesitate. She burst through the front door, not caring what consequences may lie ahead. Alicia needed help and Nicky was determined to come to her aid. She charged into the living room, blindly pushing past the dining room furniture in her haste. Adrenaline surged through her veins and filled her with strength.

She had to save Alicia, whatever the cost.

And Delilah.

Nicky could hear Alicia screaming for help and saw that the man in the hoodie was trying to strangle her. Without hesitation, Nicky rushed up behind him, holding her gun on him.

"FBI! Stop!" she shouted.

The man turned to Nicky with wild eyes, still holding Alicia. He was a wiry figure, standing at about 5'7" with slight shoulders and arms. His skin was pale and dotted with small, dark red scars from his teenage years. His chin was pointed and his cheek bones were sharp and prominent, while his dark eyes were framed by a mop of red hair. The overall effect was one of a slightly sinister, yet desperate expression.

He didn't say a word--just kept attacking Alicia, who screamed, "Help!"

Nicky had her gun trained on them, but she couldn't get a clear shot. She could shoot Alicia if she missed.

So she did the only thing she could think of: She rushed forward and grabbed the man's arms, pulling him off of Alicia. He struggled against her grip, but Nicky held on tightly and managed to get him to the ground.

She pinned his arms behind his back, pressing her knee into his spine as she reached for the handcuffs on her belt.

But it wasn't over.

He thrashed beneath her, still not making a sound.

With a final, desperate thrust upwards, he rolled under her and plunged towards Nicky.

He was surprisingly strong and managed to free one of his hands. He spun around, lunging at Nicky with a sudden weapon. It was a piece of broken glass, jagged and sharp.

Nicky barely had time to react as the man lunged forward, aiming for her stomach. She quickly sidestepped, dodging the attack and pushing him away. She went to shoot, but he slashed at her arm--she narrowly avoided the cut, but the gun flew from her hands and slid across the floor.

The killer stumbled back, but not before Nicky saw a flash of recognition in his eyes. He knew who she was--he had been expecting her all along.

At that moment, Nicky knew, without a doubt, that this was him.

The man who'd been sending her the recordings.

The man who took Delilah.

But Delilah wasn't here. She just prayed she wasn't too late.

He dove at her. Nicky ducked, but he was surprisingly agile. He grabbed her by the throat and squeezed, his eyes wild with rage. Nicky gasped for breath, struggling to break free as his grip grew tighter and tighter. She felt lightheaded, fear coursing through her veins as she fought against him.

Nicky saw her chance and launched with all her strength, her foot meeting his knee with a sickening crunch. He stumbled back, but she knew he would not be down for long. In a desperate bid for freedom she dove for the gun, but he caught her with a crashing tackle. Furniture flew as they struggled, hands grasping, searching for the advantage. Nicky felt his iron-like grip encircle her throat and the air was sucked from her lungs as he squeezed with all his might. She fought to break free, but his hands held tight.

Nicky's lungs burned as the last gasp of air escaped her throat and her vision blurred around the edges. His hands were clamped tightly around her neck, and she felt like she was back in the lake house all those years ago, submerged beneath frigid water, barely able to keep her head above the surface. She could almost hear the murky liquid threatening to swallow her whole, and then the memory of that night hit her like a thunderclap - leaving her breathless and overwhelmed by a fear that no words could describe.

She thought of him: the kidnapper, the man who had taken her life and threatened her family. Who had kept Rosie, long after Nicky got away.

Her attacker.

That man...

For the first time, Nicky remembered something about him.

His face.

She had never gotten a good look at it, but she remembered the bottom of his face. The wrinkles in his twisted smile. And his long nose.

She saw him, enough to recognize a feature or two. Enough that if she saw him in person, she might actually know who he aws.

And in that moment, she felt an overwhelming sense of rage and urgency.

Nicky's adrenaline spiked--she had to get this man off of her. She had to escape. She had to do whatever it took to save herself.

Before she could, something shattered. He stumbled back, releasing his grip on Nicky's throat. Nicky gasped for air and took in the scene before her.

Alicia had just hit him over the head with a heavy vase from nearby, sending shards of glass flying across the room.

Nick staggered back, coughing and sputtering as she tried to catch her breath. The man was on the floor, wheezing and clutching his head in pain as Alicia ran up to Nicky's side.

"Are you okay?" she asked frantically.

Nicky nodded and took a deep breath, turning to the man on the floor. He was still conscious, but looked dazed and confused.

And so was Nicky.

With her head light, she looked around for her gun. "My gun," she said. "Where is it?"

She spotted it underneath a chair.

Nicky felt a surge of adrenaline as she prepared to take the leap. But, just as she was about to make her move, she noticed a strange absence. She quickly looked up, and the man was gone. The front door of the house was wide open, and Alicia let out a scream.

"He ran away!

Panic slammed into Nicky. No! she couldn't let him escape--he still had Delilah!

She dove for her gun and grabbed it, then sped out of the house faster than she ever had.

Up ahead, she saw him running up the dark street, toward a group of commercial buildings.

Nicky's heart raced as she chased after him, gun in hand. He had a good head start, so Nicky pushed herself to run faster, not letting even a second go by without her giving chase.

She ran and ran until her lungs burned and her legs ached, but still she kept going. She had to catch this man--she had to save Delilah and make sure he never hurt anyone else ever again.

She ran after him, pushing past her own exhaustion and adrenaline as she kept up with his long strides.

She spotted the man turn a corner into an alleyway and followed, gun drawn in her shaking hands. She was so close to the truth she could feel it.

Finally, she could find out if Delilah was okay.

But she had to catch him first.

Nicky zipped into the alleyway, but stopped the moment she arrived.

Parked in the alleyway was a car.

A small sedan, parked alone, as if waiting just for her. The moonlight shone down on it, illumining the alley in a silvery hue.

There was no sign of the killer anywhere. At least, not at first glance.

Then, Nicky heard movement. And she realized that the back door of the car was open.

The man dragged someone out, into the alleyway.

A woman, bound by ropes, with duct tape over her mouth.

And red hair.

Delilah.

And he had a knife pressed to her throat.

CHAPTER TWENTY SIX

Jarred smiled as he looked into the FBI agent's eyes, feeling a deep satisfaction with himself. He couldn't speak--he had no voice--but still, he had been heard.

Agent Nicky Lyons had followed him here, all the way from Jacksonville, Florida, to Wahoe Bay, Bahamas.

She'd listened to his recordings.

She'd uncovered his clues.

She'd heard him.

And now she was here.

He knew she would be worth it.

He grinned at her as he held a knife to Delilah's throat, facing off against her in the alleyway. In person, Nicky had a tall and domineering energy; her long brown hair was tied back, and she glared at him with intense brown eyes, pointing her gun straight at him.

But he knew she wouldn't shoot.

He had Delilah, and Nicky Lyons--based on what he'd read of her on the news--was not the type of woman to simply let a victim die.

No, he had the upper hand here.

He would win.

"Let her go, you bastard," Nicky demanded, but Jarred simply smiled. He pressed the knife deeper onto Delilah's throat, and the woman squirmed beneath him, unable to make much more than a peep beneath the duct tape on her mouth.

Panic flitted across Nicky's face. He grinned. This was how he could communicate with her. He couldn't speak, but she'd understand his movements.

"Don't," Nicky said. "Don't do it."

He relaxed the knife, to show her he wouldn't--if she cooperated.

"What do you want?" Nicky asked, but her gun was still on him. He needed that gone. "Can you not speak?"

He shook his head. Then, he pointed to the cuffs on Nicky's belt with his free hand.

"What about them?" Nicky asked.

He gestured to Delilah, then gestured to Nicky. He wanted her to cuff herself to Delilah, to bind them together.

"Are you crazy?" Nicky asked. "I have a gun on you. Drop the weapon."

He shook his head with a smile, as if taunting her and saying, *"I know you won't shoot."* He pressed the knife down on Delilah again, and Nicky finally gave it up. He could see the realization in her eyes. She was going to have to choose between her gun and Delilah's life.

"Okay, okay," she said, raising her hands and the gun. "I'll put it down, okay?"

He smiled again, a bit wider this time. He nodded and gestured to the ground. Nicky slowly lowered her gun to the ground, then kicked it away from them. Relief flooded through Jarred. Now, he had the upper hand again.

He gestured to her cuffs once more.

Nicky hesitated for a moment before finally relenting and reaching for the handcuffs. She cuffed one end around her wrist, then pulled Delilah's arm up and fastened it around hers as well.

Jarred let out a sigh of relief as he eased his grip on Delilah's throat and stepped back, keeping his knife trained on them both as Nicky stood there with her hands bound together with Delilah's. He could see the fear in their eyes but also a spark of determination in Nicky's gaze that hadn't been there before--a spark that told him she wasn't giving up yet.

He picked up Nicky's gun and held it on them, a warning that he'd shoot if she tried to run. It would be impossible with Delilah's legs bound anyway, and he knew the agent wasn't going to let the girl die.

Too bad for both of them.

They were going to die anyway.

With a cruel smile, he went into the back of his car, still holding the gun on them, and pulled out a cannister of gasoline.

This was going to be his public speech.

Everyone would soon know his name.

CHAPTER TWENTY SEVEN

Nicky watched in horror as the madman poured gasoline in a wide circle around her and Delilah, the liquid pooling in shapes like a thick river around her feet. The gasoline's acrid stench overwhelmed Nicky's senses, mixing with the metallic and chemical odors of the air, enveloping her and clinging to her hair like a toxic cloud.

There she was, literally attached to a very alive Delilah Roberts--but not for long.

If he lit a match, then they would both go up in flames.

She had to think fast. But he had her gun. One wrong move, and he could shoot them. But she also didn't have time to think.

She needed to get out of these damn cuffs and take this bastard down. If she broke her thumb, she might be able to get her hand out, but it wasn't going to be easy.

He kept dumping more gasoline.

She had to be buy time.

"You," she said, hoping to get his attention. "How did you find out where I lived? How did you get my information?"

He momentarily stopped pouring the gas. He tossed the cannister to the side, then looked at her with her gun pointed right at them, a deranged look in his eyes. She knew he wouldn't answer--he was obviously mute, but if she kept talking, she might be able to buy enough time to break free.

She brought pressure down on her hand, getting ready to pull with all her might. The pain would be excruciating, but she had to do this.

Or else it would mean death.

Not only for Delilah, but for Nicky too.

"And why did you pick me?" Nicky continued. "Why did you want me to come here?"

But the man didn't reply. He just stared at them with a cold, emotionless expression. Nicky knew she wasn't going to get an answer from him. He had already made up his mind and he was determined to carry out his plan.

She felt her heart sink as she realized there was no easy way out of this situation. She pulled down harder on her thumb, but breaking a finger was a lot easier said than done.

But she had to do it.

She had to try.

Just as she was about to make a move, the man grabbed a match from his pocket and lit it with a flick of his wrist. Nicky felt her heart stop in her chest as he brought the flame closer to them.

Her mind raced as she watched him bring the match closer and closer. There had to be something she could do!

And then it hit her.

She yanked her thumb as hard as she could, feeling the bone break and skin tear as the handcuff. She quickly grabbed Delilah as the man threw the match down. Nicky pulled Delilah away, running as fast as she could out of the circle of gasoline before it could light.

The match lit the gasoline on fire in a blaze, sending flames soaring high into the sky. The heat was intense, and Nicky felt her skin start to burn as she ran faster and faster away from the danger. She shoved Delilah to the side, because at that moment--despite the danger of the flames--she knew that the man still had a gun, and he was still a threat.

The flames blazed with an intensity that washed out the darkness, setting everything in a bright orange-yellow hue. The light was so bright it felt like the sun was in the alleyway, and Nicky had to squint and shield her eyes against it. The smell of the fire was pungent and smoky, seeping deep into her lungs until she felt like she couldn't get a good breath.

Through their brightness, she saw him.

The man.

He stood there, pointing the gun at the sky in anguish. He was distracted, it seemed, mesmerized by the flames and the failure of his plan.

Nicky could use this.

The roar of the flames was deafening, like a freight train tearing through the room, thundering and echoing off the walls. The crackle of the fire was loud and oppressive, making it hard to think or focus, but Nicky had to move.

She had to act.

Nicky took a deep breath and dove towards the man, her hands reaching for the gun. He was still in shock.

But the man quickly snapped out of it and a fight broke out. Nicky and the man tussled, both of them trying to get a grip on the gun. Nicky was smaller and weaker, but she was determined and desperate. She pushed and shoved and kicked, determined to get the gun away from him.

The man was strong and powerful, but Nicky was fueled by adrenaline and the will to survive. She twisted and turned, using all her strength to try and pry the gun away from him. He thrust and pulled, trying to keep her away, but Nicky refused to give up.

Finally, with one last shove, Nicky managed to break free of his grip and the gun flew into the air. Nicky scrambled to catch it, and as she did, the man lunged towards her. Nicky caught the gun in mid-air and pointed it at him, ready to defend herself.

The man stopped in his tracks. He brazenly looked right at the gun, its barrel now pointed at him, but his eyes were dazed.

He was out of his mind.

"That's enough," Nicky said, the gun pointed at him. "You're finished."

At that moment, the sound of police sirens could be heard, rapidly approaching. Alicia must have called the cops, and Nicky hoped Ken got word too.

The man looked around, as if he was trying to figure out what to do next. Nicky kept the gun pointed at him, her heart pounding in her chest.

The sirens grew louder and louder until finally two police cars and a fire truck appeared at the end of the alleyway. Police and firemen jumped out, ready to take control of the situation. They quickly got in formation and moved towards them, guns drawn and ready for anything.

Nicky felt relief flood through her body as she saw them approach. The man had no chance now; he was surrounded by police officers and firefighters with their weapons trained on him. He slowly put his hands up in surrender, knowing that it was over for him.

Nicky glanced around at all the commotion; it seemed like they were going to be okay after all. She let out a sigh of relief as the firefighters quickly began dousing the flames with their hoses while the police cuffed the man and took him away from the scene.

Police officers came over and cuffed the man. The moment passed in a blur as Nicky watched everything unfold before her eyes; she could hardly believe that they had made it out of this alive. But they did--they survived against all odds--and she couldn't help but feel proud of herself for being brave enough to take action.

Nicky hurried over to Delilah, who was being untied by police officers. They ripped off the duct tape over her mouth, and she gasped for air. Tears streamed down her face.

Nicky stopped before her, and Delilah looked up at her with tears in her eyes.

"Y-you..." she said. "You saved me."

Nicky managed to smile. "I wasn't going to give up until I did."

Delilah began sobbing. "I didn't think anyone was looking for me."

Nicky wrapped an arm around her shoulders. "I'm so glad you're okay."

"It's okay," Nicky said, giving her a squeeze. "Everything is going to be okay now."

Nicky stood before Delilah with a grin on her face. It was over now. It was all over. They had survived against all odds, and she couldn't have been more proud of herself for saving Delilah's life.

Just then, another car pulled up to the curb at the street, and Nicky saw Ken jump out. With concern all over his face, he jogged toward them.

Nicky grabbed onto Delilah's shoulders and smiled at her. "Your family is going to be so happy to have you home. Stay with the police, Delilah. Everything's gonna be okay now."

Delilah nodded and turned to face Nicky, her eyes overflowing with gratitude.

"Thank you," she said in a soft voice. "Thank you for not giving up on me."

Nicky smiled back at her warmly and gave her a hug. "You're welcome," she said softly. She felt Delilah's body shuddering against hers as they embraced, and it was a reminder of just how close they had come to disaster tonight--and how much courage it had taken to get them out of it alive.

The police officers began ushering everyone away from the scene, but before they left, Delilah looked back at Nicky one last time and mouthed the words 'thank you' again. Nicky nodded in understanding and smiled at her reassuringly as Ken jogged up beside her.

"Hey, you okay?" he said, gently touching her arms.

Nicky looked up at Ken, overwhelmed with a surreal happiness.

She couldn't help it--she threw her arms around him, hugging him tight.

"I'm glad you're okay," he said. "How did you know where to look for her?"

"I didn't," Nicky said, pulling back from him slightly. "I just knew I had to keep looking. I wasn't giving up until I found her."

"Well, you did a great job," Ken said, giving her a smile. "I knew you could do it." Ken held her tighter, and Nicky felt safe in his arms.

Nicky felt a warmth spreading through her, and she looked up into his eyes. In that moment, everything felt right. She knew that no matter what happened next, they would be alright. Together, they had saved Delilah--and each other.

There were three more girls on their list to save, and Nicky felt more sure than ever that they could do it.

CHAPTER TWENTY EIGHT

Nicky was grateful to be back in Jacksonville, which seemed like an eternity away after the Bahamas.

She walked through the FBI headquarters, making her way to the briefing room, where she was headed to meet with the chief and her team. The morning sun seeped in through the tall windows that lined the hall, and warm rays of light slipped across her cheeks as she walked.

She'd been able to sleep well last night, knowing that she had saved Delilah's life.

Nicky was almost to the briefing room, but she hesitated when she arrived at the door. Chief Franco was waiting in there with Ken and Grace, but Nicky felt strangely nervous, because while she had done a good job on this case, there was still something heavy on her mind.

And that was the intel Fred Garrison had on Rosie's kidnapper.

Nicky paused at the door, thinking on it. Her informant hadn't texted her back about Rosie yet. Nicky didn't know what it was yet. But she wanted to ask Chief Franco, once again, if they could officially re-open Rosie's case under the jurisdiction of the FBI.

Rosie was kidnapped all the way in West Virginia, nowhere near Florida, but they were the FBI--they could tackle cases federally. Chief Franco had told her before that if she had tangible evidence there was something worth going after in terms of catching the kidnapper, then he'd consider re-opening it officially.

Nicky didn't have that evidence yet... but soon, she would. She was going to head to the prison herself to get answers.

Until then, she had to be patient. She opened up the door to the briefing room, greeted by the familiar long table and the windows that let the sun in, showing the skyline of Jacksonville.

Ken was sitting next to Grace, with Chief Franco at the head of the table. They all nodded as Nicky came in.

"Lyons, glad you could make it," the chief said, nodding.

Nicky smiled and sat down across from Ken and Grace. They both smiled at her, and Nicky nodded back.

"Great work, as usual," Chief Franco said. "You saved Delilah Roberts, and with that, we can cross another name off the list." The chief smiled at Nicky. "Lyons, you're doing a great job leading this team. Senator Gregory was right--you were the person for the job."

Nicky felt a warmth swell in her chest. She'd been working so hard, and it felt good to be recognized for it.

"Thank you, sir," Nicky replied, feeling proud. "I'm just glad I could help."

"That guy you caught was a real piece of work," the chief continued. "His name is Jarred Parker, and he's going to jail for a long time for the murder of June Peterson and the kidnapping of Delilah Roberts, as well as his attempted assault on Alice O'Conner."

Nicky pictured Jarred's face. He had been so wild and crazed, and yet he couldn't speak. There was something so chilling about that; she had seen the insanity in his eyes, and yet she hadn't been able to hear any words to understand exactly what he was thinking about.

"Why do you think he did it?" Nicky asked. "Anything in his file?"

"Well, he was born mute," the chief said, "and his mother died ten years ago. She was a redhead, like the victims."

Nicky nodded. She had theorized earlier in the case that the killer had been trying to have a voice, probably because he didn't have one. He was stealing other people's voices, and using them to get Nicky's attention.

"He was also a loner," the chief continued. "Never had any friends or family, and he was always looking for attention. We think he wanted to be noticed, and this was his way of doing it."

Nicky nodded again. It all made sense now--Jarred's motive, his strange behavior during the arrest, everything.

But one thing still didn't add up.

"How did he have my details?" Nicky asked. "Why did he pick me?"

"Well, as it turned out, Jarred was loaded," the chief said. "His mother left him behind a lot of money, and because he never had any social life or anything, he saved it all up. He hired a hacker on the black market to get your details after seeing you on the news. This whole thing has made the entire FBI nervous. If someone could hack us and find out private information about one of our agents so easily, then that's a huge breach of security. We're doing a major overhaul on our systems to ensure this can't happen again." The chief sighed. "I'm sorry, Lyons. This was a failure on our part."

Nicky shook her head. "No, sir, it wasn't," she said firmly. "We caught him, and that's what matters most. You put me in charge of this team and gave us the resources we needed to find him. I am grateful for your faith in me."

The chief smiled at her. "You're right," he said. "It takes a lot of courage to take on something like this, and you have my utmost respect for doing so." He extended his hand to Nicky and shook hers firmly. "I'm proud to have you as part of my team, Lyons."

Nicky felt a swell of gratitude towards the chief for his words of encouragement and support. She was relieved that Delilah had been found safe and sound, but more importantly, she was grateful that the chief had trusted her with such an important task. She knew that without his support, none of this would have been possible--and for that, she was truly thankful.

But she hadn't been alone. Ken had been with her every step of the way, and she nodded at him with a smile.

"Agent Walker did fine work too, Chief," Nicky said. "And Grace too. We're a team, and we work best when we're together."

The chief smiled and nodded in agreement. "Yes, you certainly do," he said. "You should all be proud of yourselves for a job well done." He paused for a moment, looking around the room at Nicky, Ken and Grace before continuing. "I'd like to thank each and every one of you for your hard work on this case," he said solemnly. "It's not often that we get such a successful outcome in cases like these, but because of your dedication and determination, justice has been served." He looked at each of them in turn, his gaze settling on Nicky last as he smiled warmly. "Thank you," he said simply before turning back to the group.

"Just doing our jobs, Chief," Ken said with a grin.

"And I barely did anything on this one!" Grace exclaimed with a sigh. "Nicky and Ken are the superstars. I'm just the girl behind the computer."

"Your job is important too, Grace," Nicky said. "We need your tech skills. You're a huge help."

"Well, I don't know about that," Grace replied, blushing slightly at the compliment. "But I'm glad I could do my part."

"Oh, you're all heroes to me," the chief said, clapping his hands together. "And you should all go home and take some time off. I'm sure you could all use it."

"Yes, sir," Nicky replied with a nod. "We appreciate you letting us stick around this long to help find Delilah."

"I wouldn't hear of you not being here," the chief replied. "I never want this family to be without the people they love."

"Thank you, Chief," Nicky said, smiling warmly.

"Don't mention it," the chief said. "Now get out of my office and get some rest."

"Yes, sir," Nicky replied with a grin.

With that, the three of them left the chief's office and made their way back down the hallway. As they walked, Nicky couldn't help but feel a sense of accomplishment and pride swell inside her. She had done it--she had found Delilah and helped bring her home safely. And she hadn't been alone in her endeavor--Ken and Grace had been by her side every step of the way.

The hallway seemed brighter now than it had before, illuminated by the sun streaming in through the windows at each end. They walked slowly, talking quietly about what their next move should be now that Delilah was safe. Nicky felt a warmth spread through her chest as Ken squeezed her hand reassuringly, while Grace walked beside them with a smile on her face. It was moments like these that reminded Nicky why this job was so special--the camaraderie between friends who worked together to solve a case was unlike anything else in life.

"Well, I'm beat," Grace said as they stood at the end of the hall. "I'm gonna go home and get some art done. What are you two up to?"

Nicky shared a look with Ken. She wanted to bring him back to her place so they could finally get some alone time. They hadn't ended up needing that hotel bed... but after everything, Nicky was ready to push their relationship just a bit further.

"Gonna take it easy," Ken said, nodding at Nicky with a knowing smile.

"Well, see ya tomorrow," Grace said as she headed down the hall.

Now alone by the elevator, Nicky leaned against the wall and faced Ken with a playful smile.

"So," she said, "you want to come see my place?"

Ken looked at Nicky with a twinkle in his eye.

"I'd love to," he said. "It's been too long since I've seen it."

Nicky smiled, her heart fluttering at the thought of Ken coming over. She had been so busy lately that she hadn't had much time for herself, let alone for a romantic evening. But now, here was an opportunity to spend some quality time with Ken and show him just how much he meant to her.

"Then what are we waiting for?" Nicky said as she grabbed his hand and led him towards the elevator. As they stepped inside, Nicky couldn't help but feel excited for what the day would bring.

***

Nicky stepped into her apartment and tossed the keys on the console table.

Ken walked in after her, looking around with curiosity, and Nicky felt her cheeks heat up.

She hadn't had many men in here. And she'd definitely never had Ken over. They spent so much time together on cases, and yet seeing him in her home made her feel nervous.

"Your place is really nice," Ken said.

Nicky smiled. Her apartment was modest, but it had a great view of Jacksonville through the windows.

"Thanks," she said, motioning for him to sit on the couch. "Can I get you something to drink? Water, soda, beer?"

Ken smiled and took a seat.

"A beer would be great," he said as he settled into the cushions.

Nicky nodded and headed towards the kitchen, her heart pounding in her chest. She had always been so good at staying composed when they were out on cases--but now that they were alone in her home, she felt like she was about to burst with excitement. She grabbed two bottles of beer from the fridge and popped off their caps before returning to the living room.

She handed Ken his bottle before taking a seat beside him on the couch. He took a sip of his beer and looked at Nicky with admiration in his eyes.

"I'm really proud of you," he said softly, setting his bottle down on the coffee table and reaching out to take her hand in his own. "You did an amazing job on this case."

Nicky blushed, feeling warmth spread through her body as Ken's thumb lightly stroked hers.

As she stared into his blue eyes, at that moment, she knew she didn't want to wait anymore.

They'd been waiting for too long.

Taking a deep breath, she leaned forward and kissed him gently on the lips. She felt Ken's mouth move against hers, his lips moving in sync with hers, and she pulled back to look at him.

Nicky could see the desire in his eyes, and she could tell that he'd been as waiting for this as much as she had.

He leaned in and kissed her again, this time more passionately. Nicky felt the warmth of his body against hers as he pulled her close and she ran her fingers through his hair. He tasted like beer and sunshine, and she felt herself melting into him as they continued to kiss.

The kiss seemed to last forever, but eventually they pulled away from each other, both breathless.

Nicky smiled at Ken, feeling happier than ever before. She had been so worried about taking the leap with him, but now that she had, it felt like the most natural thing in the world.

"I'm glad you're here," she said softly as she looked into his eyes.

Ken smiled back at her and brushed a strand of hair from her face before pulling her close for another kiss. This one was even more passionate than before, and Nicky could feel all of her worries slipping away as he held her tightly in his arms.

They stayed like that for a few minutes, just holding each other and kissing, until finally they pulled away and looked into each other's eyes. It was in that moment that Nicky knew that she had found something special with Ken, and she was so happy that she had finally taken the chance to be with him.

As they sat there, just inches apart, Nicky looked into Ken's eyes and couldn't help but smile. She knew that no matter where life took them, they would always have this moment--the moment that changed everything.

Just as they were about to get lost more, Nicky's phone vibrated on the coffee table. She didn't want to ruin the moment--but the message reminded her that she was waiting to hear back from her guy at the prison. It could be him.

She pulled away.

Ken smiled at her knowingly. "It's okay. Answer it."

"Sorry." Blushing, Nicky grabbed her phone and looked at the text, her stomach in knots--both from Ken's kiss, and from the prospect of hearing back.

The message was from the guard at the prison:

We can set up a meeting with Garrison today.

He says he has important information for you.

EPILOGUE

Nicky walked through the sterile halls of the prison. The walls were stark white, punctuated by occasional steel doors, and fluorescent lights illuminated the hallway at regular intervals. The air was stiff and oppressive, making her feel like she was being watched. Nicky heard the harsh sound of her shoes against the hard linoleum, echoing off the walls like a distant metronome. The occasional clang of metal and the mumbled conversations of guards provided a disconcerting soundtrack to her journey.

She never liked coming here, but it had to be done.

The prison smelled stale and dusty, with a hint of unwashed clothing and sweat lingering in the air. It was a stark contrast to the comforting smell of home that Nicky had left behind before entering these walls. She wished she was back at her apartment with Ken, continuing where they'd left off, but if she was able to get a meeting with Fred Garrison today, then she had to take it.

She kept walking toward the meeting room until she reached a door. Before it, she took a breath.

This might finally be what she was waiting for.

Information on the true whereabouts of her sister's kidnapper.

Fred Garrison was her criminal informant, an inmate tasked with spying on another inmate--Felix Anderson, the man who was mentored by the same guy who had kidnapped Nicky and her sister all those years ago. The same man who knew what happened to Rosie.

If Garrison finally had the information she needed, then it would be huge. She could finally bring something to Chief Franco and re-open Rosie's case for real. If Nicky had been able to save Delilah, then maybe she could save Rosie too.

Nicky opened the door and stepped inside. The room was small, but it had all the necessary amenities for a prison-room meeting: a table, two chairs, and a security camera in the corner. Fred Garrison was already there, sitting in one of the chairs with his arms crossed over his chest. He looked up when Nicky entered and gave her a slight nod.

"You made it," he said gruffly.

Nicky nodded back and took a seat across from him. "I'm here," she said, trying to keep her voice steady despite her racing heart. "What do you have for me?"

"First, I need to reiterate our deal," he said. "I want out of this hellhole. I'm not giving you the information unless you guarantee it."

"You have my word," Nicky said, and she meant that. Garrison's crimes were light, and as an FBI agent, she could easily pull some strings to get him out of here early.

If he could help bring her back to Rosie, then hell, she'd give him anything.

"Tell me what you know," Nicky said. "Please."

Her heart thrummed with anticipation. Fred sighed, then looked at her.

"Okay. I was able to pry more out of Felix."

"And..?"

The anxiety was too much for Nicky--her heart pulsed louder, and her head became light. The pressure became almost too much to bear. She felt as if she was standing right in front of an oncoming train, unable to move out of the way.

Fred paused, as if considering his words carefully. Then, he finally said, "Felix is hard to crack. I had to be really careful with my words. For a bit there, I was afraid he was onto me."

Nicky nodded, waiting for more. *Please, just tell me.*

"But I finally got something out of him," Garrison said.

He took a breath. Nicky held hers.

Then, Garrison said, "Agent Lyons, the man you're looking for is in Nelly, West Virginia. Does that mean anything to you?"

Nicky's vision blurred as her head spun. A feeling of dread clogged her chest, the weight of her anxiety pressing down on her shoulders like a ton of bricks. The ground seemed to shake beneath her feet, and the world seemed to be tilting around her.

Had he really been so close all along? She could hardly imagine it.

Nelly.

That was her hometown.

Her sister's kidnapper had been right there, under her nose the entire time.

Nicky breathed deep and tried to focus. She had to stay strong and get her emotions in check.

"Yes," she said, her voice coming out shaky. "Yes, it means something."

Garrison nodded. "I thought as much."

If this were all true, then Garrison had done the job Nicky had asked of him. He was a criminal, but as far as she was concerned, he deserved his second shot at life.

"If this is true," Nicky said, "then I'll keep my promise to you. I'll get you out of here."

Garrison's nostrils flared, and he squared his shoulders. "I was half-expecting you to screw me over."

"No," Nicky said. "I'm always true to my word. What will you do when you get out?"

Garrison shrugged. "I haven't thought that far ahead," he said. "But I think I'll be alright. I'll probably just take it day by day and see where life takes me."

She knew it was wrong to feel happy in a place like this, but it still warmed her heart to see someone like Garrison get a second chance.

Garrison stood up and held out his hand, and Nicky shook it. "Thank you," he said.

"Thank you for the information," Nicky replied. "It's been a pleasure doing business with you. I'll take it from here."

Garrison nodded, and with that, Nicky left the room. She felt a little lighter now, despite the overwhelming gravity of the situation. If Garrison's information was correct, then she was one step closer to finding out what happened to Rosie.

She felt a sense of hope she hadn't felt in years.

Nicky had a lead.

NOW AVAILABLE!

ALL IN
(A Nicky Lyons FBI Suspense Thriller—Book 8)

When another woman goes missing, matching the signature of one of FBI Special Agent Nicky Lyons' missing persons' cases, Nicky has a realization of the missing link. She knows the only way to catch this killer is to set herself up as bait—yet this time, out there all alone, Nicky may have just gone too far.

"A masterpiece of thriller and mystery."
—Books and Movie Reviews, Roberto Mattos (re Once Gone)

ALL IN (A Nicky Lyons FBI Suspense Thriller) is book #8 in a long-anticipated new series by #1 bestseller and USA Today bestselling author Blake Pierce, whose bestseller Once Gone (a free download) has received over 7,000 five star ratings and reviews.

A page-turning and harrowing crime thriller featuring a brilliant and tortured FBI agent, the NICKY LYONS series is a riveting mystery, packed with non-stop action, suspense, twists and turns, revelations, and driven by a breakneck pace that will keep you flipping pages late into the night. Fans of Rachel Caine, Teresa Driscoll and Robert Dugoni are sure to fall in love.

Future books in the series will soon be available.

"An edge of your seat thriller in a new series that keeps you turning pages! ...So many twists, turns and red herrings… I can't wait to see what happens next."
—Reader review (Her Last Wish)

"A strong, complex story about two FBI agents trying to stop a serial killer. If you want an author to capture your attention and have you guessing, yet trying to put the pieces together, Pierce is your author!"
—Reader review (Her Last Wish)

“A typical Blake Pierce twisting, turning, roller coaster ride suspense thriller. Will have you turning the pages to the last sentence of the last chapter!!!”
—Reader review (City of Prey)

“Right from the start we have an unusual protagonist that I haven't seen done in this genre before. The action is nonstop… A very atmospheric novel that will keep you turning pages well into the wee hours.”
—Reader review (City of Prey)

“Everything that I look for in a book… a great plot, interesting characters, and grabs your interest right away. The book moves along at a breakneck pace and stays that way until the end. Now on go I to book two!”
—Reader review (Girl, Alone)

“Exciting, heart pounding, edge of your seat book… a must read for mystery and suspense readers!”
—Reader review (Girl, Alone)

Blake Pierce

Blake Pierce is the USA Today bestselling author of the RILEY PAGE mystery series, which includes seventeen books. Blake Pierce is also the author of the MACKENZIE WHITE mystery series, comprising fourteen books; of the AVERY BLACK mystery series, comprising six books; of the KERI LOCKE mystery series, comprising five books; of the MAKING OF RILEY PAIGE mystery series, comprising six books; of the KATE WISE mystery series, comprising seven books; of the CHLOE FINE psychological suspense mystery, comprising six books; of the JESSIE HUNT psychological suspense thriller series, comprising twenty-eight books; of the AU PAIR psychological suspense thriller series, comprising three books; of the ZOE PRIME mystery series, comprising six books; of the ADELE SHARP mystery series, comprising sixteen books, of the EUROPEAN VOYAGE cozy mystery series, comprising six books; of the LAURA FROST FBI suspense thriller, comprising eleven books; of the ELLA DARK FBI suspense thriller, comprising fourteen books (and counting); of the A YEAR IN EUROPE cozy mystery series, comprising nine books, of the AVA GOLD mystery series, comprising six books; of the RACHEL GIFT mystery series, comprising ten books (and counting); of the VALERIE LAW mystery series, comprising nine books (and counting); of the PAIGE KING mystery series, comprising eight books (and counting); of the MAY MOORE mystery series, comprising eleven books; of the CORA SHIELDS mystery series, comprising eight books (and counting); of the NICKY LYONS mystery series, comprising eight books (and counting), of the CAMI LARK mystery series, comprising eight books (and counting), of the AMBER YOUNG mystery series, comprising five books (and counting), of the DAISY FORTUNE mystery series, comprising five books (and counting), of the FIONA RED mystery series, comprising five books (and counting), of the FAITH BOLD mystery series, comprising five books (and counting), and of the new JULIETTE HART mystery series, comprising five books (and counting).

An avid reader and lifelong fan of the mystery and thriller genres, Blake loves to hear from you, so please feel free to visit www.blakepierceauthor.com to learn more and stay in touch.

BOOKS BY BLAKE PIERCE

JULIETTE HART MYSTERY SERIES
NOTHING TO FEAR (Book #1)
NOTHING THERE (Book #2)
NOTHING WATCHING (Book #3)
NOTHING HIDING (Book #4)
NOTHING LEFT (Book #5)

FAITH BOLD MYSTERY SERIES
SO LONG (Book #1)
SO COLD (Book #2)
SO SCARED (Book #3)
SO NORMAL (Book #4)
SO FAR GONE (Book #5)

FIONA RED MYSTERY SERIES
LET HER GO (Book #1)
LET HER BE (Book #2)
LET HER HOPE (Book #3)
LET HER WISH (Book #4)
LET HER LIVE (Book #5)

DAISY FORTUNE MYSTERY SERIES
NEED YOU (Book #1)
CLAIM YOU (Book #2)
CRAVE YOU (Book #3)
CHOOSE YOU (Book #4)
CHASE YOU (Book #5)

AMBER YOUNG MYSTERY SERIES
ABSENT PITY (Book #1)
ABSENT REMORSE (Book #2)
ABSENT FEELING (Book #3)
ABSENT MERCY (Book #4)
ABSENT REASON (Book #5)

CAMI LARK MYSTERY SERIES
JUST ME (Book #1)
JUST OUTSIDE (Book #2)
JUST RIGHT (Book #3)
JUST FORGET (Book #4)
JUST ONCE (Book #5)
JUST HIDE (Book #6)
JUST NOW (Book #7)
JUST HOPE (Book #8)

NICKY LYONS MYSTERY SERIES
ALL MINE (Book #1)
ALL HIS (Book #2)
ALL HE SEES (Book #3)
ALL ALONE (Book #4)
ALL FOR ONE (Book #5)
ALL HE TAKES (Book #6)
ALL FOR ME (Book #7)
ALL IN (Book #8)

CORA SHIELDS MYSTERY SERIES
UNDONE (Book #1)
UNWANTED (Book #2)
UNHINGED (Book #3)
UNSAID (Book #4)
UNGLUED (Book #5)
UNSTABLE (Book #6)
UNKNOWN (Book #7)
UNAWARE (Book #8)

MAY MOORE SUSPENSE THRILLER
NEVER RUN (Book #1)
NEVER TELL (Book #2)
NEVER LIVE (Book #3)
NEVER HIDE (Book #4)
NEVER FORGIVE (Book #5)
NEVER AGAIN (Book #6)
NEVER LOOK BACK (Book #7)
NEVER FORGET (Book #8)
NEVER LET GO (Book #9)

NEVER PRETEND (Book #10)
NEVER HESITATE (Book #11)

PAIGE KING MYSTERY SERIES
THE GIRL HE PINED (Book #1)
THE GIRL HE CHOSE (Book #2)
THE GIRL HE TOOK (Book #3)
THE GIRL HE WISHED (Book #4)
THE GIRL HE CROWNED (Book #5)
THE GIRL HE WATCHED (Book #6)
THE GIRL HE WANTED (Book #7)
THE GIRL HE CLAIMED (Book #8)

VALERIE LAW MYSTERY SERIES
NO MERCY (Book #1)
NO PITY (Book #2)
NO FEAR (Book #3)
NO SLEEP (Book #4)
NO QUARTER (Book #5)
NO CHANCE (Book #6)
NO REFUGE (Book #7)
NO GRACE (Book #8)
NO ESCAPE (Book #9)

RACHEL GIFT MYSTERY SERIES
HER LAST WISH (Book #1)
HER LAST CHANCE (Book #2)
HER LAST HOPE (Book #3)
HER LAST FEAR (Book #4)
HER LAST CHOICE (Book #5)
HER LAST BREATH (Book #6)
HER LAST MISTAKE (Book #7)
HER LAST DESIRE (Book #8)
HER LAST REGRET (Book #9)
HER LAST HOUR (Book #10)

AVA GOLD MYSTERY SERIES
CITY OF PREY (Book #1)
CITY OF FEAR (Book #2)
CITY OF BONES (Book #3)

CITY OF GHOSTS (Book #4)
CITY OF DEATH (Book #5)
CITY OF VICE (Book #6)

A YEAR IN EUROPE
A MURDER IN PARIS (Book #1)
DEATH IN FLORENCE (Book #2)
VENGEANCE IN VIENNA (Book #3)
A FATALITY IN SPAIN (Book #4)

ELLA DARK FBI SUSPENSE THRILLER
GIRL, ALONE (Book #1)
GIRL, TAKEN (Book #2)
GIRL, HUNTED (Book #3)
GIRL, SILENCED (Book #4)
GIRL, VANISHED (Book 5)
GIRL ERASED (Book #6)
GIRL, FORSAKEN (Book #7)
GIRL, TRAPPED (Book #8)
GIRL, EXPENDABLE (Book #9)
GIRL, ESCAPED (Book #10)
GIRL, HIS (Book #11)
GIRL, LURED (Book #12)
GIRL, MISSING (Book #13)
GIRL, UNKNOWN (Book #14)

LAURA FROST FBI SUSPENSE THRILLER
ALREADY GONE (Book #1)
ALREADY SEEN (Book #2)
ALREADY TRAPPED (Book #3)
ALREADY MISSING (Book #4)
ALREADY DEAD (Book #5)
ALREADY TAKEN (Book #6)
ALREADY CHOSEN (Book #7)
ALREADY LOST (Book #8)
ALREADY HIS (Book #9)
ALREADY LURED (Book #10)
ALREADY COLD (Book #11)

EUROPEAN VOYAGE COZY MYSTERY SERIES

MURDER (AND BAKLAVA) (Book #1)
DEATH (AND APPLE STRUDEL) (Book #2)
CRIME (AND LAGER) (Book #3)
MISFORTUNE (AND GOUDA) (Book #4)
CALAMITY (AND A DANISH) (Book #5)
MAYHEM (AND HERRING) (Book #6)

ADELE SHARP MYSTERY SERIES
LEFT TO DIE (Book #1)
LEFT TO RUN (Book #2)
LEFT TO HIDE (Book #3)
LEFT TO KILL (Book #4)
LEFT TO MURDER (Book #5)
LEFT TO ENVY (Book #6)
LEFT TO LAPSE (Book #7)
LEFT TO VANISH (Book #8)
LEFT TO HUNT (Book #9)
LEFT TO FEAR (Book #10)
LEFT TO PREY (Book #11)
LEFT TO LURE (Book #12)
LEFT TO CRAVE (Book #13)
LEFT TO LOATHE (Book #14)
LEFT TO HARM (Book #15)
LEFT TO RUIN (Book #16)

THE AU PAIR SERIES
ALMOST GONE (Book#1)
ALMOST LOST (Book #2)
ALMOST DEAD (Book #3)

ZOE PRIME MYSTERY SERIES
FACE OF DEATH (Book#1)
FACE OF MURDER (Book #2)
FACE OF FEAR (Book #3)
FACE OF MADNESS (Book #4)
FACE OF FURY (Book #5)
FACE OF DARKNESS (Book #6)

A JESSIE HUNT PSYCHOLOGICAL SUSPENSE SERIES
THE PERFECT WIFE (Book #1)

THE PERFECT BLOCK (Book #2)
THE PERFECT HOUSE (Book #3)
THE PERFECT SMILE (Book #4)
THE PERFECT LIE (Book #5)
THE PERFECT LOOK (Book #6)
THE PERFECT AFFAIR (Book #7)
THE PERFECT ALIBI (Book #8)
THE PERFECT NEIGHBOR (Book #9)
THE PERFECT DISGUISE (Book #10)
THE PERFECT SECRET (Book #11)
THE PERFECT FAÇADE (Book #12)
THE PERFECT IMPRESSION (Book #13)
THE PERFECT DECEIT (Book #14)
THE PERFECT MISTRESS (Book #15)
THE PERFECT IMAGE (Book #16)
THE PERFECT VEIL (Book #17)
THE PERFECT INDISCRETION (Book #18)
THE PERFECT RUMOR (Book #19)
THE PERFECT COUPLE (Book #20)
THE PERFECT MURDER (Book #21)
THE PERFECT HUSBAND (Book #22)
THE PERFECT SCANDAL (Book #23)
THE PERFECT MASK (Book #24)
THE PERFECT RUSE (Book #25)
THE PERFECT VENEER (Book #26)
THE PERFECT PEOPLE (Book #27)
THE PERFECT WITNESS (Book #28)

CHLOE FINE PSYCHOLOGICAL SUSPENSE SERIES

NEXT DOOR (Book #1)
A NEIGHBOR'S LIE (Book #2)
CUL DE SAC (Book #3)
SILENT NEIGHBOR (Book #4)
HOMECOMING (Book #5)
TINTED WINDOWS (Book #6)

KATE WISE MYSTERY SERIES

IF SHE KNEW (Book #1)
IF SHE SAW (Book #2)
IF SHE RAN (Book #3)

IF SHE HID (Book #4)
IF SHE FLED (Book #5)
IF SHE FEARED (Book #6)
IF SHE HEARD (Book #7)

THE MAKING OF RILEY PAIGE SERIES
WATCHING (Book #1)
WAITING (Book #2)
LURING (Book #3)
TAKING (Book #4)
STALKING (Book #5)
KILLING (Book #6)

RILEY PAIGE MYSTERY SERIES
ONCE GONE (Book #1)
ONCE TAKEN (Book #2)
ONCE CRAVED (Book #3)
ONCE LURED (Book #4)
ONCE HUNTED (Book #5)
ONCE PINED (Book #6)
ONCE FORSAKEN (Book #7)
ONCE COLD (Book #8)
ONCE STALKED (Book #9)
ONCE LOST (Book #10)
ONCE BURIED (Book #11)
ONCE BOUND (Book #12)
ONCE TRAPPED (Book #13)
ONCE DORMANT (Book #14)
ONCE SHUNNED (Book #15)
ONCE MISSED (Book #16)
ONCE CHOSEN (Book #17)

MACKENZIE WHITE MYSTERY SERIES
BEFORE HE KILLS (Book #1)
BEFORE HE SEES (Book #2)
BEFORE HE COVETS (Book #3)
BEFORE HE TAKES (Book #4)
BEFORE HE NEEDS (Book #5)
BEFORE HE FEELS (Book #6)
BEFORE HE SINS (Book #7)

BEFORE HE HUNTS (Book #8)
BEFORE HE PREYS (Book #9)
BEFORE HE LONGS (Book #10)
BEFORE HE LAPSES (Book #11)
BEFORE HE ENVIES (Book #12)
BEFORE HE STALKS (Book #13)
BEFORE HE HARMS (Book #14)

AVERY BLACK MYSTERY SERIES

CAUSE TO KILL (Book #1)
CAUSE TO RUN (Book #2)
CAUSE TO HIDE (Book #3)
CAUSE TO FEAR (Book #4)
CAUSE TO SAVE (Book #5)
CAUSE TO DREAD (Book #6)

KERI LOCKE MYSTERY SERIES

A TRACE OF DEATH (Book #1)
A TRACE OF MURDER (Book #2)
A TRACE OF VICE (Book #3)
A TRACE OF CRIME (Book #4)
A TRACE OF HOPE (Book #5)

Made in United States
Troutdale, OR
02/14/2025

28972393R00099